THE
Enid Blyton™
BEDTIME
BUNNY BOOK

**BLOOMSBURY
CHILDREN'S
BOOKS**

This edition first published by Bloomsbury Publishing Plc in 2000
38 Soho Square, London, W1V 5DF

These stories were first published in
The Adventures of Binkle and Flip by George Newnes 1938

Enid Blyton™

A CIP catalogue record of this book is available from the British Library
ISBN 0 7475 4785 8

Printed in Dubai by Oriental Press

1 3 5 7 9 10 8 6 4 2

THE
Enid Blyton™
BEDTIME
BUNNY BOOK

A collection of Binkle and Flip stories

Illustrated by Jill Newton

BLOOMSBURY
CHILDREN'S
BOOKS

Introduction

These comforting stories reveal the world of Binkle and Flip, two rascally rabbits who seem to end up in all kinds of muddles – and often with a lot of explaining to do! You can guarantee that when Herbert Hedgehog finds himself in a rather prickly situation the naughty rabbits aren't far away, and when a mysterious whistling Biggle-Boggle suddenly arrives in the woods, who do you think is responsible? But worst of all, on the special day King Otter pays a rare visit to Oak Tree Town, just how does Binkle manage to offend him in front of all the other townsfolk? Binkle and Flip might be sneaky, but their tricks are nearly always discovered, leaving them feeling very guilty – and sorry for themselves. But don't worry, it's never long before they dream up yet another scheme! Although the residents might not entirely agree, Oak Tree Town would be a far less exciting place without Binkle and Flip. So why don't you choose a story and snuggle up to share the fun and antics of two mischievous rabbits and numerous animal friends in your *Enid Blyton Bedtime Bunny Book*.

Contents

CHAPTER 1

The Whistling Biggle-Boggle

Oak Tree Town was terribly upset. Little Bobs Bunny had disappeared the week before and nobody knew where he had gone to. And now Minny Mouse, one of Creeper Mouse's little daughters, had gone.

'What *can* have happened to her?' wailed Creeper in despair.

'And what *can* have become of poor little Bobs?' sighed Bess Bunny, his mother.

Sammy Squirrel came up and joined the group.

'I think I know what has become of him,' he said sadly. 'I am afraid that family of Polecats who have just come to live near Bramble Dell have had a great deal to do with the disappearance of Bobs Bunny and Minny Mouse.'

'Oh dear, dear!' said Dilly Duck. 'I'm afraid of Polecats!'

'What can we do about it?' asked Herbert Hedgehog.

'Let's go and tell Wily Weasel and see if he knows what to do,' suggested Mowdie Mole.

The others thought that was a very good idea, and soon everyone trooped off to Wily's.

He was very concerned about it.

'But it's no good, I can't do anything,' he said. 'We don't know for *certain* that Pippit and Pinkie Polecat have caught Bobs and Minny. The only thing I can suggest is that we think of some idea to make the Polecats go away.'

Just at that moment Flip and Binkle Bunny strolled up. Wily Weasel saw them.

'Hey, Binkle!' he called. 'Come here a minute.'

'What for?' asked Binkle nervously. 'I haven't done anything naughty for ages.'

'Well, here's a chance to put your brains to work for a good cause,' said Wily. 'You're always having ideas of some sort – ideas that lead you into trouble. Now, if you can think of an idea to make Pippit and Pinkie Polecat go away from Bramble Dell, we should all be very grateful!'

Binkle began to smooth his long whiskers and perk his ears up. He felt very proud to have Wily Weasel talking to him like that.

'Well, young Bobs Bunny was my favourite nephew,' he said, 'and to punish Pippit Polecat for catching him, I will certainly think of some idea. Meet me at my Uncle Rob the Rabbit's shop tomorrow, and I will have a wonderful idea all ready to tell you.'

Then he took Flip's arm and marched away with him, leaving the people of Oak Tree Town gaping after him in admiration.

'Flip and Binkle Bunny aren't always good, but they *are* clever,' said Dilly Duck, who hadn't many brains herself, and knew it.

'They're more mischievous than bad,' said Bess, Binkle's sister. 'Well, well! We shall see if Binkle has thought of an idea by tomorrow.'

All the folk at Oak Tree Town went home and waited anxiously for the next day.

Binkle shut himself up in his bedroom, and thought and thought and thought.

Presently a smile came over his face and his nose twitched. He opened the bedroom door and called out to Flip.

'Hey, Flip!' he shouted. 'Do you know what a Biggle-Boggle is?'

'A Biggle-Boggle!' exclaimed Flip in astonishment. 'No, I don't. What is it?'

'Ha! ha!' chuckled Binkle, disappearing into the kitchen and getting some paper and a pen out of a drawer. 'You'll know soon enough, Flip.'

And not another word would the provoking Bunny say. He just sat in the kitchen and wrote something that he wouldn't let Flip see.

Next day he and Flip went down into Oak Tree Town and walked into Rob Rabbit's shop. Everyone was there waiting for them in Rob's big room at the back.

'Good morning,' said Binkle cheerfully. 'Hope I haven't kept you waiting.'

'Have you thought of an idea?' demanded Wily Weasel.

'Yes, I have,' answered Binkle, 'and if I can't get Pippit and Pinkie Polecat away from Bramble Dell in a day or two, I'll cut off my lovely whiskers!'

'Tell us your idea, quickly!' begged Sammy.

'Well, listen,' said Binkle, carefully shutting the door and lowering his voice.

Then in the middle of a breathless silence he began to tell them his plan.

'First of all, I want this notice I've written out to be copied and pasted all over Oak Tree Town and Bramble Dell,' he began, and he spread out the notice for them to see. It was a most peculiar one:

LOST

A WHISTLING
BIGGLE-BOGGLE
DANGEROUS TO
POLECATS AND FOXES
IF FOUND, PLEASE RETURN TO
GRUNZLE
AT OAK TREE TOWN HALL

'A Biggle-Boggle!' gasped everyone. 'What's that?'

'And who's Grunzle?' asked Sammy Squirrel.

'Flip is,' explained Binkle, to Flip's immense astonishment.

'Oh, *am* I!' exclaimed Flip. 'And what are you going to be?'

'Never mind that,' said Binkle. 'You'll know sooner or later. All you've got to do is to sit in the town hall and pretend you're waiting for a Biggle-Boggle to turn up.'

'Tell us more about your plan,' said Sammy, who was beginning to see what Binkle was going to do.

'No,' said Binkle firmly. 'I shall tell nothing else, in case somehow or other it leaks out and everything's spoilt. You must leave the rest to me. There's only one thing to remember. If any-one asks about Biggle-Boggles, say they're very dangerous.'

The others had to be content with that, and each of them promised to copy out one of the notices and paste it up. Then they all went home.

Next day all over Oak Tree Town appeared large notices about the lost Biggle-Boggle. An extra large one was pasted up in Bramble Dell, where Pippit and

Pinkie Polecat often went for walks.

Flip Bunny went to the town hall, dressed like a showman. He had cream trousers, a red coat, a bendy hat, and fine tall boots. He felt very proud of himself indeed.

Binkle didn't appear. He had gone off by himself with a ten pence whistle, and wouldn't tell Flip anything. He was thoroughly enjoying himself.

'Now, listen!' he said to Flip before he went. 'Just you remember every single thing I've told you about Biggle-Boggles, Flip.'

Well, Flip hadn't sat in the town hall very long before there was a great commotion in the street outside, and Pippit Polecat rushed into the hall.

'Are you Grunzle?' he asked Flip. 'Well, what's this about Biggle-Boggles? What are they?'

'They're fat creatures,' explained Flip, remembering all Binkle had told him. 'And they love to dance in the moonlight among the trees and whistle to the moon. They live in China, generally.'

'Well, how did this Biggle-Boggle come *here*?' demanded Pippit, who didn't like the sound of them at all.

'I brought it back from China,' said Flip calmly. 'I'm a showman!'

'You've no *business* to bring Biggle-Boggles back from China,' scolded Pippit. 'Why are they dangerous to Polecats and Foxes? Aren't they dangerous to anyone else?'

'Oh, *no*!' answered Flip, pretending to be astonished. 'They're very fond of everyone except Polecats and Foxes. But they have two favourite meals – one is fried Fox's brush, and the other is stewed Polecat tail. That's why I put that bit about danger in my notice. I shouldn't like my Biggle-Boggle to be put in prison for catching you and eating your tail.'

'Oh my!' said Pippit in dismay. 'Nor should I! I do hope it won't come anywhere near our home.'

He went off sadly, wondering what to do about it. No sooner had he got home and told his wife all that Flip had said, than he heard something which made him jump and turn pale from his whiskers to his tail.

It was a peculiar whistling sound! It came from the trees just beyond their house.

'Oh!' gasped Pinkie, 'it's the Biggle-Boggle! Pippit! Whatever shall we do?'

'It won't come *here*!' said Pippit bravely. 'Cheer up! I'll go and tell Grunzle later on that his Biggle-Boggle is near here, and perhaps he'll come and catch him.'

When at last the whistling stopped and Pippit thought everything was safe, he rushed once more into Oak Tree Town and went anxiously to Flip.

'Your Biggle-Boggle's near our house,' he said. 'We heard him whistling. Come and get him.'

Flip stood up and put on his hat. He walked off with Pippit till they came to Bramble Dell. Then he pretended to search and search, but nothing did he find except – Binkle!

'Have you seen anything strange about here?' asked Flip, pretending not to know Binkle.

'Yes, a peculiar fat creature that whistled,' said Binkle. 'He asked me if I knew of any Polecats round about here.'

'Ow! ow!' shrieked Pippit, and dashed into his house at once and slammed the door.

Flip and Binkle went off giggling. Pippit came to the town hall no more that day.

But that night, when he looked fearfully out of his bedroom window, he heard a whistling noise again. And there, dancing in the moonlight among the trees, he saw what looked like a peculiar fat creature!

'Oh, dear, dear! It's the Biggle-Boggle!' he said in terror. 'Whatever shall I do? I must certainly get Grunzle to catch him tomorrow.'

After a time the Biggle-Boggle stopped dancing and whistling, and disappeared among the trees, and Pippit and Pinkie went shivering to bed.

Next day Pippit went to Flip again and told him what he had seen.

'Do come and catch him!' he begged.

Flip looked grave.

'I don't think I dare,' he said. 'When he starts dancing like that it means that he's made up his mind to have one of his favourite meals. I daren't catch him till he's had it. He might bite *me*!'

'Oh dear!' groaned Pippit. 'Whatever are we to do?'

'Cheer up! He'll be all right when he's had stewed Polecat tails,' said Flip cheerfully.

Pippit howled in despair and rushed out of the hall, pulling his whiskers in the greatest alarm.

Nothing more was heard of him that day and Flip got rather tired of doing nothing. But when evening came, Binkle walked jauntily into the town.

'Hallo! Aren't you playing at being the Biggle-Boggle?' asked Flip.

Binkle didn't answer.

'Call the folk of the town together,' he commanded.

Flip did so.

'Come with me,' said Binkle, when they were all there, and he led them to Bramble Dell.

He stopped just near the Polecats' cottage and pointed.

'Look,' he said.

They all looked. A big notice was hanging from a tree in the garden:

THIS COTTAGE TO BE LET

it said!

'It's empty!' said Binkle. 'Pippit and Pinkie Polecat have gone away for good.'

'Hurrah! hurrah!' shouted the folk of Oak Tree Town. 'Three cheers for Binkle and the Biggle-Boggle.'

And they hurried Binkle and Flip back to the town as fast as they could. In half an hour Mowdie Mole and Dilly Duck had got a lovely feast ready in the town hall, and Wily Weasel told Binkle to sit at the head and Flip at the foot.

Didn't they feel proud!

And at the very end, Wily Weasel stood up and said, 'We are very glad that Binkle and Flip Bunny have done Oak Tree Town a good turn at last. I hope they will never be naughty any more.'

But I'm afraid that was rather too much to hope for.

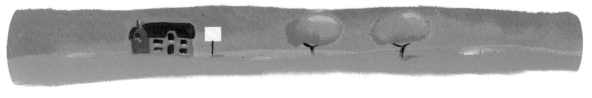

CHAPTER 2

Binkle Tries to Be Funny

One day Flip came in from his shopping and found Binkle sitting in a corner of the garden with a wet towel tied round his head. He held a pencil in one paw and a piece of paper in the other. His nose was going up and down faster than Flip had ever seen it before.

'Binkle,' cried Flip, 'what's the matter? What have you got that towel round your head for? Have you hurt yourself?'

Binkle sniffed.

'Go away, Flip,' he said, 'I'm writing poetry.'

Flip sat down on the garden path in astonishment.

'Writing poetry!' he squeaked. 'I didn't know you could. Anyway, what's the point of it, Binkle, and why have you bandaged your head?'

'Poets always do,' answered Binkle crossly. 'And I'm writing it because I've got an idea that people will buy my poems.'

Flip was so certain that they wouldn't that he got up and went indoors without saying another word. But as he was getting the salad ready for dinner, he began to wonder what Binkle's poetry was like.

He put his head out of the window.

'Hey, Binkle!' he said. 'Come and read me your poem!'

Binkle looked round and grinned.

'All right,' he said, and got up. He came indoors, and stood on a stool to read his poem. He looked very funny with the towel still round his head, and Flip wanted very badly to laugh. But he was afraid of upsetting Binkle, so he waited.

'Ahem, ahem,' coughed Binkle, pulling at his whiskers proudly. Then he began:

'To Dilly Duck
'There never was a nicer Duck
Than darling Mistress Dilly,
She's always most polite and kind,
And never rude or silly.

'Her beak is shining just like gold.
Her heart is golden too,
Oh, Mistress Dilly, there's no doubt
I think a *lot* of you!'

Binkle stopped.

Flip stared at him in astonishment.

'Oh, Binkle,' he exclaimed excitedly, 'fancy you writing that! It's *awfully* good. I've never heard better poetry, really I haven't! What are you going to do with it?'

'Send it to Dilly Duck with my very best wishes,' said Binkle, smiling in delight at Flip's admiration. 'I'll put it in an envelope now, and you can take it.'

Flip scratched his ear and looked at Binkle. 'But what did you write that about *Dilly* for?' he asked. 'I thought poets wrote about flowers and stars and things.'

'Well, I'll tell you,' said Binkle, busily pushing his poem into a very large envelope, and licking it down. 'Dilly Duck is very vain and she'll be so pleased with this that she'll show it to everybody. And *everybody* will want poems written about them. And I shall make them pay fifty pence a time, and get a lot of money.'

'Binkle, you *are* clever!' said Flip. 'I couldn't have thought of that, and I couldn't have written the poems either, if I'd thought of the idea. I think you're a genius.'

'I think I must be a bit of one,' answered Binkle modestly, as he wrote Dilly's name on the envelope.

Flip ran off with the envelope and soon arrived at Dilly Duck's post office. He knocked at the door, and slipped the letter into the letter-box. Then he went away, chuckling to think what Dilly would say when she opened the envelope.

Dilly waddled to the door and took the letter from the box. Then she went back to her kitchen, put on her glasses, and opened the letter.

'To Dilly Duck,' she read.

'Bless my beak, it's a poem!' she cried in astonishment, and sat down excitedly in her big armchair.

She read the poem out loud all the way through. Her feathery throat heaved with excitement.

'Well, I never! A poem all about me, by Binkle Bunny. He's a bad bunny, but he's got a good heart, and he must be clever to write this about me! What *will* everybody say?'

She read the poem through again. When she came to the piece 'Her beak is shining just like gold,' she got up and looked at herself in the mirror.

'Fancy him noticing that,' she said in delight. 'I must really have this framed. Dear, dear, dear, *what* an excitement to be sure.'

Dilly looked in her cupboard and found a little red frame that just fitted the poem. She proudly put it in, and then, going into her little office, she hung it up on the wall where anyone who came in could see it.

After a little while Mowdie Mole came in to buy a stamp. She saw the poem hanging in its frame on the wall, and bent closer to read it.

'To Dilly Duck!' she read, and looked at Dilly. 'My goodness gracious, who's been writing a poem to you?' she gasped in great surprise.

'Binkle Bunny,' answered Dilly, shaking her tail feathers in excitement. 'It's an awfully good poem, Mowdie, so true and so beautifully *put*.'

Mowdie read it through and turned to look at Dilly's yellow beak.

'Well, I never!' she said. 'I'd be proud if I had a poem like that written about me, Dilly Duck. Look, here's Sammy Squirrel from next door. Let's show him the poem.'

Sammy read it and was most astonished. He thought it very good indeed, and Dilly grew more and more delighted. Sammy said he'd fetch Herbert Hedgehog to see what *he* thought of it. He went out into the street to fetch him and brought back Riggles Rat as well.

Soon the shop was full of people reading Binkle's poem. Nobody there had ever tried to write poetry, and they thought it was simply wonderful.

Herbert Hedgehog took it down from the wall, sat down in a chair, and read it very slowly out loud. Then he said something that everyone else was thinking.

'Why did Binkle write this poem to *Dilly*, and not to anyone else?' he wondered.

'I suppose he likes me best,' she said, 'and anyway, I'm the only one with a beak. Perhaps *that's* what made him write it.'

By evening, everybody in Oak Tree Town knew about Binkle's poem to Dilly. And everyone thought, 'I wish I could have a poem written about *me*.'

The more Mowdie Mole thought of it, the more she wanted one. And at last she determined to go and ask Binkle if he would write her one.

So off she trotted that evening, making sure no one was looking where she went. She soon arrived at Heather Cottage and knocked at the door.

Flip opened it.

'Come in,' he said, and Mowdie Mole walked into the kitchen, where Binkle was sitting with a towel tied round his head again.

'He's making poetry,' explained Flip in a whisper. 'He says poets always have to sit with wet towels round their heads.'

'Fancy that!' whispered Mowdie Mole, all in a flutter to see Binkle making poetry, and wondering whether it was about *her* this time.

After a time Binkle sighed very deeply and looked up.

'Oh, good evening, Mowdie Mole,' he said. 'It's very, very kind of you to pay us a visit.'

'Well, you see, I saw that poem about Dilly Duck,' explained Mowdie Mole nervously. 'I *did* so like it. It was beautiful – and I wondered if you would write one for me, I *would* love it so!'

Binkle pulled his fine whiskers.

'Poetry's very hard work,' he said solemnly. 'I'm afraid I would have to charge you fifty pence for it.'

'I'd be glad to pay,' said Mowdie, putting her hand into her pocket and bringing up fifty pence. She put it on the table.

'Very well,' said Binkle, putting the coin in his pocket just before Flip got to it. 'I'll send the poem tomorrow. Goodbye. I can feel the poetry coming again.'

He made a face and groaned.

Mowdie Mole fled out of the room. 'I'm glad I don't write poetry,' she whispered to Flip. 'It looks as if it hurts dreadfully.'

No sooner had Flip shut the door than he had to open it again, this time to fat Herbert Hedgehog.

'Where's Binkle?' he asked.

'In the kitchen, making poetry. Sh!' answered Flip.

Herbert Hedgehog looked rather scared.

'I – I don't think I'll go in,' he said. 'Is it a sort of disease?'

'Yes, I think it must be,' answered Flip, thinking of Binkle's groans. 'He got it quite suddenly.'

'Well, I think his poetry about Dilly was wonderful,' said Herbert, 'but I don't think I want to catch the disease. Give him this pound and ask him to send me a poem about myself, will you? Don't tell anyone.'

Flip wriggled his nose and chuckled.

'I won't tell,' he promised, and let Herbert Hedgehog out of the front door. Binkle was tremendously pleased when Flip told him about the pound.

'I shall charge a *pound* for my poems, then,' he said, 'instead of fifty pence, as people want them

so badly.'

He wrote the poems for Mowdie Mole and Herbert Hedgehog, and Flip took them round. They were both most delighted with them. Mowdie Mole's went like this:

Mowdie Mole is very neat
From her nose unto her feet,
She has eyes so black and bright,
They can pierce the darkest night,
And her ears are nice and small,
I think I like them best of all.

Herbert Hedgehog was so excited over his that he went down the street reading it out loud, so that everyone could hear.

'Herbert Hedgehog's a good old fellow,
  He lives in a house that is painted yellow,
  His prickles are long and sharp and brown,
  He's very well known in Oak Tree Town.
  He's rather fat and he's certainly funny.
  This poem is written by Binkle Bunny.'

He wasn't quite certain if he liked the bit about his being fat and funny, but he thought it was so lovely having a poem written all about himself, that he felt as if he couldn't mind *anything*.

By this time all Oak Tree Town was getting very excited over Binkle's poems. Everybody determined to get Binkle to write a poem for him – or herself, and Flip was kept very busy answering the door to people who came to ask for Binkle.

Binkle enjoyed it all immensely. He sat in the garden or in the kitchen, always with a towel round his head, because that seemed to astonish people very much. He had given up having it wet, because it gave him a cold and he found it hard to write poetry properly when he kept sneezing.

He was quite willing to write poems for anyone who liked to pay for them.

Nearly everyone in Oak Tree Town came and asked him for one, for nobody could bear to be left out. It became quite the fashion to have the poems framed and put up over the mantelpiece, and when you went to tea with anyone the first thing you did was to read the poem, and say, 'Very nice. Oh, very nice *indeed.*'

One day Wily the Weasel came to Heather Cottage. Binkle was sitting in the garden as usual with the towel round his head. When he saw the policeman of Oak Tree Town coming in the gate, he got up hurriedly and scuttled indoors. He wasn't at all sure whether Wily had come for a poem, or to scold him for something naughty he had done at some time or other.

But Wily had come for a poem. He didn't like Binkle for he felt he was a very bad bunny, but he couldn't bear to be the only one who hadn't a poem about himself.

'Hey, Binkle!' he called. 'Will you write me a poem?'

'Certainly,' answered Binkle, putting his head out of the window. 'That will be five pounds.'

'Don't be silly,' answered Wily. 'I'll give you fifty pence, and you'll do it for that, or I'll remember something bad you've done and come in and scold you. Here's fifty pence. Catch it.'

Binkle bristled his whiskers, caught the fifty pence piece, and wished he dared say something rude. A sudden thought came to him, and he grinned.

'All right, Wily,' he called. 'I'll send the poem tomorrow.'

All that night he made it up and, when it was finished, he copied it out neatly. Then he crept through Oak Tree Town to where Wily Weasel lived, and pinned the poem up on the door. Then he ran back, chuckling.

When Wily Weasel was having breakfast next morning, he and his wife heard laughing and talking going on outside. When he peeped out of the window, he saw a crowd of folk looking at something on his door.

'Come out and read your poem, Wily,' they called. 'It's a *lovely* one!'

Wily opened the door and saw the piece of paper pinned on it. This is what he read:

> 'Wily Weasel came to me,
> Yesterday, just after tea,
> And asked if I would kindly write
> A little poem, nice and bright,
> To say how kind he is, and wise,
> And how we like his pretty eyes,
> And how we'd love to kiss his nose,
> And watch his dainty twinkling toes.
> But all that I can *truly* write
> About our policeman on this night,
> Is how I hope he'll catch a measle,
> For I don't like Wily Weasel!'

Wily Weasel was furiously angry. He knew that all Oak Tree Town would hear of Binkle's joke and enjoy it, and he tore the paper down, in a great rage.

He raced up to Heather Cottage, determined to punish Binkle. But

Binkle was ready for him and the doors were bolted. Binkle poked his head out of the window.

'Have you come for another poem?' he asked politely.

'How *dare* you write like that about me?' raged Wily.

'Oh, didn't you like it?' asked Binkle in great surprise, sticking his big ears up straight. 'Well, I didn't want to write it, you know – you made me do it. I can't help what poetry comes into my head, can I? You shouldn't have made me do it for you.'

Wily went off angrily, feeling it really *was* his own fault.

But, dear me, Oak Tree Town didn't bother at all about whose fault it was. They enjoyed the joke thoroughly and thought Binkle not only clever, but funny.

Binkle began to think he was too, and started writing funny poems that weren't very kind. Then things began to go wrong for him. It happened like this.

Oak Tree Town heard that Oll the Otter, who was King of Runaway River, beyond Bracken Hill, was coming to visit Oak Tree Town. They were very excited about it.

'What can we do to give him a good welcome?' they cried.

'I know,' said Herbert Hedgehog, thinking of his framed poem at home. 'Let's get Binkle to write a poem about Oak Tree Town to present to Oll the Otter. That will make him very pleased, and he will think what clever people we must be here. We'll tell Binkle to put in lots of nice things about us.'

'Good idea, good idea!' cried everyone, patting Herbert Hedgehog on the back till he choked.

Sammy Squirrel was chosen to go and ask Binkle. He set off that very evening and found Flip and Binkle both in the garden.

Sammy didn't take long telling Binkle what Oak Tree Town wanted.

'And mind you say lovely things about everyone,' he said, 'and you'll have two pounds.'

'All right,' said Binkle, very pleased. 'What will I get if I say things that *aren't* lovely, Sammy?'

'Nothing at all,' said Sammy crossly. 'So don't try any tricks like you tried on Wily Weasel, Binkle.'

Sammy went home and left the two bunnies alone. Binkle looked

rather mischievous, and Flip began to be afraid he was going to do something naughty.

'Binkle,' he begged, 'tie your towel round your head and begin writing a *lovely* poem. Please, oh please, don't write anything bad!'

Binkle loved teasing Flip. He smoothed his whiskers and chuckled.

'Go away, Flip,' he said. 'I'll read you what I've written when it's done.'

Now Binkle meant to write a fine poem, but he also thought it would be rather fun to write a naughty one just to shock Flip. So he set to work on the two poems, while Flip watched him anxiously from the kitchen window.

When they were done he went indoors.

'Here you are, Flip,' he said, giving him the naughty poem. 'Do you think that will do?'

This is what Flip read:

'Your Majesty, please will you hear,
This verse by Binkle Bunny,
Who welcomes you to Oak Tree
    Town
And all its people funny.
Let me tell you who we are,
Here's a Hedgehog vain,
And here's a Badger and a Duck
Who're both extremely plain.

Then there's Wily Weasel,
How we wish he'd go!
Don't be friendly with him,
He isn't nice to know.'

When Flip had read as far as this, his knees began to shake and he sat down on a chair.

'Binkle!' he groaned. 'I can't bear it. It's unkind. We'll be turned out of Oak Tree Town.'

'The end's all right,' chuckled Binkle, twitching his ears in delight, and taking the poem from Flip. 'Listen!

'The only persons in this town
Who're really worth your trip,
Are Binkle, with his whiskers fine,
And naughty little Flip.'

Flip would have torn up the whole poem if he could have got it, but Binkle wouldn't let him. So Flip went to bed very miserable, while Binkle stayed up and copied out his good poem in his best writing.

Oll the Otter was coming the next day and Binkle was to read his welcoming poem in the Town Hall just before the feast held in honour of King Otter's arrival.

When the time came, he dressed himself carefully, and let poor Flip into the secret of his other poem.

'The other poem's fine!' he laughed. 'You wait till you hear it'.

Flip was very relieved. He was never quite certain what Binkle would do.

Binkle stuffed his poem into his pocket and set off with Flip. They had just taken their places on the platform when Oll the Otter arrived, very pleased to find such a welcome awaiting him.

When he heard that a poem was to be read, he was still better pleased. He thought poetry was tremendously clever.

Binkle, feeling very important, pulled out his poem, and, just a

little nervous, began to read it.

'Your Majesty, please will you hear,
This verse by Binkle Bunny,'

he began.

'Who welcomes you to Oak Tree
    Town,
And all its people funny.
Let me tell you who we are,
Here's a Hedgehog vain . . .'

Binkle suddenly stopped and gazed at his poem in horror.

He had put the wrong one in his pocket! Whatever was he to do? His nose twitched nervously and he blinked his eyes. Everybody stared.

'It's – it's the wrong poem,' he stammered at last.

'Oh, never mind,' said Oll the Otter graciously. 'I like any poetry, and I don't mind a bit what it's about. Go on.'

'I don't think I can,' said Binkle, pulling his whiskers so hard that one long one came out. 'The right one's at home. Flip, go and fetch it!'

'Well, while Flip is gone, read me *that* one,' said Oll the Otter, growing very curious to hear it.

There was nothing for Binkle to do but read it. He felt simply dreadful, for no one spoke a word all the time, and he was nearly crying when he reached the end.

'H'm, not very funny, and very unkind,' said Oll the Otter. 'I think you deserve a scolding, and hope you'll get it.'

'He certainly will,' said Wily Weasel, coming forward and taking hold of Binkle by his collar. He was hurried out of the hall and locked up in a shed.

Flip soon came back, and Wily Weasel read the proper poem to Oll the Otter, who thought it very good.

'It's a pity he doesn't always write like that,' he said. 'I should scold him, but not too much. And I shouldn't encourage him to write any more. He can't be trusted.'

Then they all sat down to the feast and thoroughly enjoyed themselves; except poor Flip, who couldn't help feeling sorry for Binkle. He squashed a lettuce into his pocket to give him afterwards.

Binkle got his scolding, but not too much, and when he went home with Flip he felt very sorry indeed that he had been silly enough to spoil his day.

'If you hadn't tried to be too clever, you'd have been a lot happier,' said Flip, giving him his lettuce.

CHAPTER 3

'Swee-ee-eep!'

Is there any food in the cupboard, Binkle?' asked Flip, opening one eye and looking at Binkle, who was dressing.

'No, there isn't as you well know!' snapped Binkle, who was in a very bad temper. 'You just jump out of bed, you lazy thing. We've got to *work* today, if we want any food to eat!'

'Oh, oh!' groaned Flip. 'I do hate work! Whatever can we do, Binkle?'

'We must think,' said Binkle. 'Listen! Who's that calling outside?'

He went to the window and leaned out.

Brock Badger the Sweep was outside, carrying his poles and brushes over his shoulder.

'Sweeeep! Sweeeep!' he called, in his deep, husky voice. Then he caught sight of Binkle at the window.

'Chimneys swept, Binkle?' he asked.

'No!' answered Binkle, and Brock went off, crying, 'Sweeeep!' again over Bumble Bee Common.

Binkle watched him.

'Flip,' he said, 'come here!'

Flip came to the window.

'See old Brock!' said Binkle. 'He gets a good lot of money by sweeping chimneys. And there's nothing much in it! Just fix your poles together, swish the brush up the chimney, and there you are!'

'Sounds nice and easy!' said Flip, watching Brock Badger knock at

27

Slippy Stoat's door in Briar Bank.

'It is easy,' said Binkle, 'and what's more, we'll do it, Flip! We'll borrow Brock's poles and brushes, and go off to Bracken Hill Town away yonder, and sweep all the chimneys we can! My! We'll come back with our pockets full of money!'

'But how can we get Brock to lend us his brushes?' asked Flip doubtfully. 'Nobody round here trusts us much, you know.'

'Wait and see!' answered Binkle cheerfully. 'Come on! There goes Brock over the Common. Let's catch him up.'

The two rabbits scurried downstairs and ran over the Common. They couldn't see which way Brock had gone, so Flip went down Heather Path and Binkle ran down Hazel Road.

After a bit, Binkle smelt smoke, and he peered round a tree and found Brock Badger cooking his breakfast. It smelt very good. Binkle watched Brock with his bright brown eyes, and wondered how he could get him to lend his poles and brushes.

Brock finished his breakfast, kicked out the fire, and lit his pipe, leaning back against a tree.

Gradually his eyes closed, his pipe fell from his mouth, and he began to snore loudly.

Binkle grinned. He knew how he was going to borrow Brock's brushes now!

He stole round the tree, picked up Brock's bundle, slung it over his shoulder, and ran off, chuckling.

'My!' said Flip, meeting him at a bend in Hazel Road. 'How on earth did you get Brock to lend you his things, Binkle?'

'He didn't say no, and he didn't say yes,' chuckled Binkle, 'so I just took them! He was sound asleep, Flip!'

'Well, we'll have to give them back when we've finished with them,' said Flip nervously. 'We don't want Wily Weasel the policeman after us, you know!'

'Stuff and nonsense!' laughed Binkle. 'Come on! We'll make a lot of money today in Bracken Hill Town, Flip. We'll give Brock a fine dinner for lending us his brushes, when we come back!'

Off the two went, and after a long walk arrived at Bracken Hill Town.

'Wweeeep!' shouted Binkle. 'Wweeeeep! Here, Flip! I can't shout and carry these things! You carry them and then I can shout properly!'

Flip took them, grumbling, and Binkle began to shout in a most tremendous voice.

'*Sweeee-eep! Sweeeeeep!* Twenty-two chimneys swept yesterday – what do you think of *that*, folks? Sweeeep! Finest sweeps in the world! Sweeeep!'

'Binkle! We'll get into trouble if you say we're the finest sweeps in the world,' began Flip hurriedly. 'Everyone'll *know* we're not!'

'Be quiet, Flip! How are they to know? And, anyhow, we *might* be the finest sweeps out! You can't tell till you've tried!' said Binkle in a fierce whisper.

Flip said no more, but followed Binkle, carrying the poles and very much hoping that no one wanted chimneys swept that morning. He felt extremely nervous about it.

Bushy Squirrel knocked at her window-pane. Binkle looked up and pulled his cap off politely.

'Sweep your chimney, ma'am?' he called.

'Yes!' answered Bushy. 'It's been smoking terribly this morning. You've just come along in time. But don't make more mess than you can help, will you?'

Binkle and Flip went into the little house. It only had one chimney, so they couldn't make any mistake about sweeping the right one.

Binkle began fixing the poles together, and pushed the first one up the chimney, with the brush fixed well on.

Suddenly the brush reached something hard and wouldn't go any further. Binkle pushed and pushed, but it was no good.

He pulled down the brush and put his head up the chimney to look.

Then he reached his paw up and tried to feel what it was. It was a brick fallen down, blocking up the chimney so that the smoke couldn't go up properly.

Binkle twisted the brick about until he got it loose enough, and then, turning it sideways up, he neatly lifted it down the chimney.

'Say, Flip,' he whispered, 'this chimney doesn't need sweeping! This brick stopped it up!'

'Shall we go and tell Bushy Squirrel?' said Flip jumping up.

'Rather not!' said Binkle, scornfully. 'Pack up the poles and brushes, and leave this to me, Flip!'

Whilst Flip was busy tying up the bundle, Binkle got paper and wood and laid a fire. He lit it, and when it was crackling merrily, with the blue smoke going up the chimney, he called Bushy Squirrel.

She came running in.

'Have you finished already?' she asked in surprise.

'Your chimney is perfectly all right now,' said Binkle, waving his hand towards the crackling fire. 'See, we have lit a fire for you to show you that the chimney doesn't smoke. And we haven't made a mess of your room at all, have we?'

'Well, well, well!' marvelled Bushy, holding her paws up in astonishment. 'Not a mite of soot anywhere, and all so quickly done too. You certainly *are* marvellous sweeps!'

Just then someone went by the window. Bushy ran to it and leaned out.

'Mary Mole!' she called. 'Mary Mole! Just come in here a minute and see what I've had done!'

Mary Mole came waddling in, and was delighted to see how wonderfully clean the sweeps had kept the room.

'My bedroom chimney badly wants sweeping,' she said. 'Could you come and do it now? I was going to let Brock the Badger do it, but he is not as clean or as quick as you are.'

'Certainly, ma'am!' answered Binkle, shouldering his poles. 'We'll come now. We charge a pound, please, for sweeping chimneys,' he said, turning to Bushy Squirrel.

'Very cheap – very cheap!' said Bushy, feeling for her purse. Binkle wished he had said two pounds, but it was too late to change.

Then Flip and Binkle followed Mary Mole to her house in the middle of the village. She took them up to her little blue-and-white bedroom.

'Here you are,' said she. 'I *am* so glad I heard of you. Brock Badger always makes such a dreadful mess, though he *does* try hard not to. I have to cover up everything in the room with sheets when he comes!'

She left the room and went downstairs. Flip began fixing the poles together and Binkle sat in a chair near by and watched him.

'Up the chimney she goes!' he said. 'It is nice to see you doing some work, Flip. Push hard!'

The chimney was small and the brush Flip had fitted on was very big. He pushed and pushed, and suddenly it gave, and slipped up the chimney with a rush, quite overbalancing Flip.

At the same moment a great cloud of soot fell down into the hearth and completely covered him. It flew all over the white room and settled everywhere. Binkle leaped up and began to choke and cough.

'You idiot!' he cried angrily. *'That's* not the way to sweep a chimney!'

'You should have swept it yourself, then!' choked Flip, trying to wipe himself clean, but making himself blacker still.

'Let's find the bathroom!' said Binkle. 'We can't go out like this! No one will give us work!'

They went into the bathroom near by, and turned on the taps. But instead of making themselves clean, they made the bathroom terribly dirty. The bath was streaked with black, and the floor

was covered with soot. When they dried themselves, the towels looked terrible with great black marks and smudges.

'Binkle,' said Flip, looking at his towel in dismay. 'Whatever will Mary Mole say! She *will* be angry with us!'

'This all comes of you trying to sweep a chimney!' scolded Binkle. 'Next time I'll do it. Look here, we'd better slip out of the house quietly when Mary Mole isn't looking.'

The two scamps tiptoed out of the bathroom, wrapped up their bundle of poles, and leaned over the banisters to see if Mary Mole was anywhere about.

'Listen! She's ironing in the kitchen!' said Binkle. 'We can slip out of the front door without being seen!'

So the two rabbits crept downstairs and slipped out of the front door as quietly as they could.

'Thud-thud!' went Mary's iron, and they heard her humming a little song. Poor Mary! Whatever would she say when she went upstairs!

Binkle and Flip went down the road very quietly, not daring to call out 'Sweeep!' until they were well out of Mary's hearing. When they had turned two corners and were well into an old part of Bracken Hill Town, they felt safer.

'Big houses here!' said Binkle, glancing round. 'We could get quite a lot of chimneys to sweep, I expect. Swee-ee-eep! Swee-ee-eep!'

A housekeeper mouse came running out of a big house and beckoned to them.

'Hey!' she called. 'Sweep! Sweep!'

Binkle and Flip went up to her.

'Oh!' she said, disappointed. 'I thought you were Brock Badger the Sweep. He was supposed to be coming to our house this morning to sweep the chimneys, and he hasn't come!'

'Can't we do them instead?' asked Binkle politely. 'I saw Brock Badger fast asleep off Hazel Road this morning, so I expect he's forgotten.'

At that moment the lady of the house, Binnie Badger, came out.

'Where's my cousin Brock?' she asked. 'I always let him sweep the chimneys because he's my cousin. Still, perhaps *you'd* better come and do it. If Brock can't remember, he must go without the job. Come along!'

She led the way indoors. Flip and Binkle followed, grinning at each other.

Binnie took them into the big sitting-room. Dust-sheets covered the furniture, and everything was ready for the sweep. She left them there, and they began to unpack the poles and brushes once more.

'*I'm* going to sweep the chimney this time!' said Binkle firmly. 'We can't have an awful mess like last time!'

'All right!' said Flip. 'I'm sure I don't want to sweep! It's a nasty, dirty job!'

He sat down on a chair to watch Binkle. Binkle was very busy. Up the chimney went the brush, and pole after pole was fitted neatly on. Soon there were very few poles left.

'I wonder if the brush has reached the top of the chimney yet,' said Binkle suddenly with a sigh. 'It's jolly hard work pushing and pushing, and it gets heavier each time I fix another pole on. How do you tell when the brush has reached the top, do you suppose, Flip?'

'I don't know!' said Flip. 'Perhaps, if I went outside and looked, I could see if the brush was sticking out of the chimney!'

'No, you mustn't do that!' said Binkle. 'Bushy Squirrel might come along and see you, and then we should get into a row!'

He fixed another pole on and pushed. 'Oh dear!' he sighed. 'I do wonder if it's at the top yet! It would be *so* silly if the brush was sticking ever so far up into the air, wouldn't it, Flip?'

Then Flip had an idea.

'Can't I go up on the roof and see!' he said. 'I expect there's a skylight up in an attic somewhere that I can squeeze through.'

'Yes, that's a fine idea!' said Binkle, very pleased. 'Go on up now, Flip.'

So Flip made his way upstairs, and soon came to a little attic. In the ceiling was a slanting skylight. Flip put a chair underneath, stood on it, and opened the skylight. Then he climbed through it, and there he was, on the roof.

'Goodness!' said Flip, holding on to a chimney near by. 'What a lot of them! Now I wonder which chimney Binkle's sweeping.'

He looked carefully all round. None of the chimneys seemed to have a brush sticking out.

'That's funny!' said Flip. 'I suppose Binkle's not made the brush long enough yet. Well, I'll sit down and wait till I see the brush come out, and then I'll go down and tell him.'

He sat down by a chimney and waited. It was very dull. Soon he stopped watching the chimneys and looked away over the countryside. There was a hill in the distance, and someone was running quickly down it, in the direction of Bracken Hill Town.

'That person's in a hurry!' said Flip, watching him. 'I wonder who he is!'

Flip wouldn't have stayed quietly on the roof if he *had* known who it was. It was Brock Badger hurrying to his cousin Binnie's house to explain how it was he hadn't been to sweep the chimneys as he had promised. He had been looking for his lost brushes all morning!

Brock Badger hurried down the street and at last reached Binnie's big house. He went in at the back way and found Binnie in her kitchen helping her housekeeper mouse to do some washing.

'Well, Brock Badger!' she exclaimed. '*This* is a fine time of the day to come! Wait until I put this pan of water on the fire to boil, and then I'll hear what you've got to say.'

She and the little mouse put the heavy pan of water on the fire. Then Binnie turned to Brock.

'My brushes were stolen!' he said. 'That's why I couldn't come. But I'll do your chimneys when I get them back, Binnie.'

'It's too late,' said Binnie. 'I've got two sweeps now, doing them. They're in the sitting-room.'

Binkle was certainly in the sitting-room, still fitting on poles; but Flip was where we left him, up on the roof. He had become very tired of waiting for the brush to appear.

'I'll just peep down one or two chimneys and see if I can see it anywhere,' he decided.

The chimneys were so tall that he had to climb up them before he could look down. He had just climbed up to look in a pair of chimneys, when something dreadful happened!

The brush suddenly jerked out of the one he was balancing himself on, and pushed him head first down the one he was looking into!

Poor Flip! Down the chimney he went, into the sooty darkness, trying to catch at something to stop himself. But he couldn't – and then SPLASH!

He had fallen straight into the pan of water that Binnie had put on the kitchen fire!

Splutter-splutter! What a to-do there was! Binnie and the little mouse shrieked and ran behind the door. Brock jumped up in amazement and hauled poor choking Flip out of the pan.

'What do you mean by this?' he demanded sternly. 'You're paid to *sweep* chimneys, not to fall down them like that!'

Flip blinked his eyes open and saw Brock!

'Oh! Oh!' he cried, thinking Brock had found out that he and Binkle had stolen his brushes. 'Forgive us, Brock! We didn't mean to take your brushes!'

'Oh! Oh!' said Brock, taking hold of Flip by the scruff of his neck. 'So it was you two, was it? Where's Binkle? In the sitting-room, I suppose!'

Now, Binkle had heard this to-do in the kitchen, and, creeping out, he had seen poor Flip captured. He knew he would be caught next, so he determined to run whilst he had the chance.

He raced out of the front door – straight into the arms of Wily Weasel, the policeman!

Mary Mole was with him.

When she found what a dreadful mess the two sweeps had left in her house, she went straight to Wily and told him. He promised to find the scamps for her, and just as they were walking down the road, making enquiries, Mary had seen the brush sticking out of Binnie's chimney-pot!

So of course she and Wily rushed up to the front door just in time to catch Binkle!

The two bad rabbits cried and said they were terribly sorry – but Wily said he knew their wicked ways and he took them off to lock them up.

He gave them a good scolding, and made them clean Mary Mole's house from top to bottom. Then he gave them another scolding, just for luck, and sent them off.

'We *will* be good now!' said Flip sorrowfully.

'Yes – till the next time you're naughty!' said Wily Weasel with a grunt.

And he was just about right!

CHAPTER 4

The Wonderful Doctor

Binkle and Flip were just finishing their breakfast, when the postman came.

Rat-a-tat!

'Goodness! That's the postman!' cried Binkle. 'A letter for us – fancy that! I don't believe we've had one for a year.'

He ran to the front door and picked up the letter that lay on the mat.

> *Binkle Bunny*
> *Heather Cottage*
> *Bumble Bee Common*

was the address on the envelope.

'How exciting!' said Flip, when Binkle came running back with the letter. 'Who's it from?'

Binkle opened it. It was not a very long letter.

'Listen!' he said. 'It's from my uncle, Rob the Rabbit. He keeps a chemist's shop in Oak Tree Town, just opposite Sammy Squirrel's.'

Then he began to read the letter.

> *Dear Binkle* (it said),
> *I have not been well and I must go away for some time. I know you want work. Would you like to come and look after my shop whilst I am away? Then*

I need not shut it up. Let me know soon.
Your loving
Uncle Rob.

Flip and Binkle looked at one another. Then Binkle stood up and twirled his fine whiskers.

'Of course!' he said. 'Yes, I'll look after your shop for you, Uncle Rob. Binkle and Flip selling medicine and pills! My word, what fun! What do you say to the idea, Flip?'

'Can we sell medicine and pills properly?' asked Flip nervously. 'We've never done it before, you know. I shouldn't like to get into trouble over it. We always seem to be getting into trouble somehow.'

'Well, we get out of it too,' said Binkle. 'Don't be so timid, Flip! Come on! Let's make ourselves tidy, and go and see Uncle Rob.'

So the two rabbits washed and cleaned themselves, mended the holes in their shirts, patched up their trousers and then marched out over Bumble Bee Common looking very spruce and tidy indeed.

They went down Hazel Road till they reached Oak Tree Town. Then they went straight to Rob the Rabbit's shop. It was shut and the blinds were down.

Binkle knocked at the door. Rob Rabbit opened it.

'Come in,' he wheezed. 'I'm glad to see you.'

Binkle and Flip walked in and sat down.

'We got your letter,' said Binkle, 'and we've come to say we'll be pleased to look after your shop till you come back. What's the matter with you?'

'I've got a dreadful cold,' said Rob Rabbit, coughing, 'and it won't go away. So I'm going to stay with my cousin, Bibs Bunny, till it's better.'

Binkle looked round the shop. He saw a great array of bottles, boxes and jars. On one bottle he read:

'Buy this! It's a certain cure for colds!'

He picked it up.

'Why don't you take some of your own medicine?' he asked curiously. 'Look, it says, "certain cure for colds".'

'Won't cure *mine!*' said Rob shortly. 'Mine's too bad. Now look, and I'll explain things to you.'

He took them round the shop and showed them oils and ointments, pills and powders, medicines and mixtures of all kinds.

'They're quite harmless,' he

said, 'so if you do make a mistake, it won't much matter. The poisonous medicines I've put away in a cupboard. I can't have you running any risks. Business is bad enough as it is.'

'Oh, is it?' asked Binkle. 'Well, it looks as if Sammy Squirrel's chemist shop was doing well, just opposite.'

'It is,' said Rob Rabbit, with a sigh. 'I'm old-fashioned, I suppose. I can't think of any new ideas like Sammy does!'

'Well, never mind,' said Binkle, who had already got the beginnings of a very fine idea himself. 'Go away, and get better. You can safely leave the business with us, you know.'

So Rob took his bag, said goodbye, and went to stay with his cousin away in Bracken Hill Town.

Flip and Binkle sat down and looked at each other.

'Now look here, Flip,' said Binkle excitedly. 'I've got a fine idea for making this business go well! All we want is to make people curious so that they'll come in here and buy things.'

'What do you mean?' asked Flip, who was always rather afraid of Binkle's ideas.

'I'm going to wrap you up in a big black cloak and an old hat,' said Binkle, 'and I'm going to sit you down just here at the back of the shop where everyone will see you when they come in.'

'Whatever for?' gasped Flip, in great surprise.

'Why, when people come in for anything, and ask who you are, I'm going to say, "Sh! He's a wonderful doctor. He's just come from a far-off country, where he's been making whiskers grow on folk who've never had any, and tails grow thick and long, and beaks shine like gold".' Binkle grew very excited.

'Well, that is silly,' said Flip decidedly. 'I'm not a doctor, and what's the good of pretending? I couldn't do all those things.'

'No, but I could sell the medicine you make which *might* do all those things,' cried Binkle. 'Oh, don't you see? We'll have our shop crowded full, and old Sammy over there won't have any customers at all!'

'All right,' sighed Flip. 'I'll do what you say.'

Binkle rushed about making all sorts of preparations. He pulled down a big black velvet curtain and draped it round Flip. He found an old hat and put it on his head, pulled forwards over his eyes. Then he sat him on a chair at the back of the shop.

'Now we're nearly ready,' he chuckled. He printed some large labels, and put them in a heap on the counter until he would be ready to use them. He filled a number of bottles with green medicine, then some with red, and some with yellow.

Then he opened the shop door and pulled up the blinds. In the window he put a card which said:

THIS SHOP IS UNDER NEW
MANAGEMENT
COME IN AND SEE

Everybody who passed by read the card. Herbert Hedgehog was very interested, and so was Dilly Duck. Little Timothy Mouse spelt it out to his mother, and Mowdie Mole stopped to put on her spectacles to read it.

Presently the doorbell clanged and someone came in. It was Creeper Mouse the Postman,

with a letter for Rob Rabbit. But as soon as he caught sight of Flip in his black velvet cloak sitting silently at the back of the shop, he jumped, dropped the letter and fled out of the shop.

'Goodness, Flip,' chuckled Binkle, 'see what you've done!' He peeped out of the door and saw Creeper Mouse talking to Slippy Stoat.

'Yes,' Creeper was saying, 'I'm sure it's a wizard, or something, sitting at the back of the shop there. You go in and see, Slippy.'

Slippy, who was not afraid of anyone, walked up the street and into the shop. He stared in astonishment at Flip.

'Good morning,' said Binkle, from behind the counter. 'What can I do for you?'

'Who's that?' whispered Slippy, pointing to Flip.

'Him? Oh, he's a powerful doctor, a friend of mine,' explained Binkle. 'He's just back from a far-off country.'

'What's he been doing there?' asked Slippy, staring curiously at Flip.

'Making whiskers grow long on the stoats and weasels, and tails grow thick on the rabbits, and beaks shine like gold on the ducks,' answered Binkle at once.

'My word!' said Slippy, pulling at his own whiskers and staring at Flip again. 'My whiskers are very poor. Could he make them longer, do you think? Shall I ask him?'

'No, no,' said Binkle hurriedly. 'He can't talk our language. I'll ask him for you.'

He went up to Flip, bowed to him, and said, 'Wirri-worra-worra?'

'Dirri-dorra-dorra,' said Flip, in a deep voice.

Binkle turned to Slippy.

'He says the red medicine will be just the thing for your whiskers,' he explained, and reached down a bottle. He pasted on it one of his labels which said:

MEDICINE FOR GROWING
LONG WHISKERS

'One pound, please,' said Binkle.

Slippy paid him the pound, took the bottle, and went out of the shop, thinking the new doctor must be a marvellous man.

On the way home he met Herbert Hedgehog and Dilly Duck. He told them all about the wonderful doctor, and showed them the bottle of red medicine.

'You'll see me with whiskers a foot long soon,' he said. 'Why don't you go and get something to make your beak shine, Dilly?'

'I will!' said Dilly, and waddled off at once, with Herbert Hedgehog.

When they got to the shop, they both stared with round eyes at Flip, who, feeling comfortable and warm in his velvet cloak, had fallen fast asleep. Binkle was there, though, very wide awake.

'Sh!' he said. 'Don't wake him. He was up all last night making a wonderful new ointment for polishing beaks and prickles!'

'Polishing beaks!' cried Dilly.

'Polishing prickles!' said Herbert Hedgehog, very pleased.

'Here it is!' said Binkle, getting down a jar of green ointment. At that moment Flip woke up and yawned.

Binkle was afraid he would say something without thinking, so he bawled across the shop, 'Wirri-worra-worra?'

'Eh?' said Flip, sitting up in surprise. Then he saw the gaping customers and remembered.

'Birri-borra-borra!' he answered, trying not to giggle, and pulling his hat further over his eyes to hide his face.

'He says the green ointment's the right thing for beaks and prickles!' said Binkle. 'One pound each. It's wonderful stuff.'

Herbert and Dilly paid up gladly, and went off with their jars of ointment, which were labelled:

OINTMENT FOR POLISHING
BEAKS AND PRICKLES

Well, they told everyone they met about the wonderful doctor in Rob Rabbit's shop. And soon all the folk in Oak Tree Town were talking about him, and the marvellous things he could do.

Tinkle-tinkle-tinkle, went the shop bell all day long. Gillie Guinea-pig came to ask if the doctor knew of something which would grow her a tail. The doctor said, 'Girri-gorra-gorra,' and Binkle explained that that meant the yellow medicine, taken three times a day, would soon grow a tail. Of course Gillie bought a bottle.

Mowdie Mole asked for whisker-growing medicine. Timothy Mouse wanted something to make his tail longer. Riggles Rat wanted something to make his ears grow the proper shape. They had been bitten badly in a fight and looked very ragged.

Binkle was very busy. He kept saying, 'Wirri-worra-worra,' to Flip, till Flip was quite tired of answering him. Also Flip wanted his dinner, and Binkle had been so busy that he hadn't had time to get any.

When the shop got fuller and fuller, and the bottles of medicine got fewer and fewer, Flip became very tired of pretending. He wished all the people would go away. Silly little Derry Dormouse, what did he want to have longer whiskers for? And Hoppety Hare, what did he want with a large tail? Wasn't his own good enough? This chemist business was very boring. It was all very well for Binkle, he was taking lots of money. It was *dull* to sit all day and have nothing to eat.

Then an idea came to Flip. He would soon get rid of all the people and then he could tell Binkle that he wanted something to eat. He jumped up from his chair, pulled his hat over his nose, and yelled at the top of his voice.

'Dorra-borra-worra-wee! Dorra-borra-worra-wee!'

Derry Dormouse screamed and fled out of the shop. So did Riggles Rat. And after one terrified look at Flip, Hoppety Hare shot through the door and was out of sight in a moment.

'Flip! Flip! Whatever's the matter?' gasped Binkle in amazement. 'You've frightened all the customers away!'

'Good job too!' said Flip crossly. 'I want something to eat. Shut up the shop till tomorrow.'

'Certainly not, just when we're doing so well,' said Binkle.

'All right! But you won't have any wonderful doctor any more,' said Flip, and throwing off his black coat, he walked into the backroom and began to look for food.

Of course Binkle had to shut up the shop then, but as he had only about two bottles of medicine left, it didn't matter much.

'We can make some more tonight,' he said. 'Old Sammy Squirrel over the road hasn't had a single customer today I don't believe.'

So that night Binkle made some more ointments and medicines from the different things in his uncle's cupboards.

'We'll have a fine time tomorrow!' he chuckled. 'You'll have to put on that black velvet curtain again, Flip. You looked splendid!'

And next morning Binkle put the shop in order, arranged all his medicines and jars in neat rows, and put Flip in his chair again, wrapped firmly up in his black cloak. Then he waited for customers.

But none came! Not one!

Binkle was puzzled. He peeped out in to the street. No one was about except Sammy Squirrel over the way.

'What's happened?' wondered Binkle. Then he saw Dilly Duck, who kept the post office next door to Sammy Squirrel's shop, come to the window of her shop, and tap on the pane to attract Sammy's attention. She had her beak tied up in flannel.

Sammy ran into the post office, and came out again after a few minutes. He walked across to Binkle.

'Do you know what's happened?' he said sternly. 'That green ointment that your wonderful doctor said would make Dilly Duck's beak shine has turned it green!'

'Goodness!' said Binkle, sitting down suddenly. 'A green beak!

And, oh dear! I suppose Herbert Hedgehog's prickles will have turned green too!'

Sammy snorted and went out again. Presently he came back.

'Riggles Rat's ill,' he said, 'and so is Hoppety Hare. Slippy Stoat's whiskers have turned red. Derry Dormouse feels sick. Mowdie Mole couldn't get to sleep all night. It seems to me that everyone you sold medicine to yesterday feels very bad indeed. And as for Herbert's prickles, you should just see them! Green as grass they are! I shouldn't be surprised if Wily Weasel the policeman doesn't come for your wonderful doctor and take him off to prison.'

'Ow!' gawped Flip in fright, as Sammy went out again to make some medicines to give to the sick folk. 'Binkle, I *knew* it was a silly idea to dress up like this! You're always having silly ideas!'

'Oh dear!' groaned Binkle. 'This is most unfortunate. I ought to have been more careful. Anyway, nobody will be poisoned, for Uncle put away all his poisons, I know.'

'Yes, and now everyone will go to Sammy Squirrel and buy all *his* medicines to make them better!' said Flip.

Binkle looked out of the shop door. 'Flip!' he cried in fright. 'Wily Weasel's coming!'

'Oh, my goodness!' yelled Flip. He dragged off the black cloak and hat, threw them into a corner and jumped behind the counter, just as Wily Weasel came marching into the shop.

'Where's that doctor?' demanded Wily in his sternest voice.

'Gone!' said Binkle, shaking with fright. 'He's run away. I think he was a bad doctor!'

'Run away, has he?' growled Wily. 'Well, it's a good thing for him that he *has*. I've come to lock him up for making the folk of Oak Tree Town ill! Let me search the shop first, to make sure that he *has* gone!'

He looked all over the shop, but saw no one but the two trembling rabbits, Flip and Binkle. He pulled out the black velvet cloak and hat and put them over his arm.

'I won't take *you* to prison,' he said to Binkle, 'though you deserve to go. But I think you only did what that bad doctor told you to. But I shall take his hat and cloak, and if ever he comes back and wants them, just send him to me, will you?'

'Y-y-y-yes!' stuttered Binkle, very glad indeed to see Wily go away. When he had gone, he turned to Flip and tried to smile.

'Never mind!' he said. 'We've come off very well. We've got all the money, and – Oh dear!'

And, it was 'Oh dear!' For there in the doorway stood Uncle Rob Rabbit, glaring at him.

'What's this I hear of you selling medicine and making Oak Tree Town ill!' he demanded. 'And what's the tale about that doctor? Oh! I know you, Binkle! You dressed up your friend and pretended all sorts of things. Come on; I'm going to give you to Wily Weasel the Policeman!'

'No! no!' begged Binkle. 'Please don't! We've got lots of money for you, Uncle – look!'

Rob Rabbit looked and could hardly believe his eyes.

'Very well,' he said, 'I won't give you away this time. But I'm going to give you both a good scolding to teach you not to play pranks like this any more.'

And he did. And what's more, he gave them a dose of his nastiest medicine too!

'Oh dear! oh dear!' sighed Binkle, as the two rabbits went sadly home. 'I think we'd better be good for a bit now, Flip – don't you?'

But they couldn't be good for very long, as you will soon hear.

CHAPTER 5

The Fair at Oak Tree Town

'I say, Flip,' cried Binkle, rushing into Heather Cottage in great excitement. 'What do you think is coming to Oak Tree Town?'

'What?' asked Flip.

'A fair!' said Binkle. 'A fair with roundabouts and swings and everything! Won't it be fun!'

'Yes, but we haven't got any money to go on the roundabouts,' said Flip dolefully.

'No, that's a pity,' frowned Binkle, and pulled at his whiskers and rubbed his nose. Suddenly he stopped and his eyes opened wide.

'Flip!' he said. 'Flip!'

'What?' asked Flip crossly. He was trying to read.

'Oh, Flip!' said Binkle again, in a voice of deepest excitement. 'Flip!'

'Stop "Flipping" me!' said Flip. 'And tell me what you want to say.'

'Flip,' said Binkle, 'I've got the most *won*derful idea I've ever had!'

'Then I'd rather you kept it to yourself,' said Flip, hurriedly folding up his newspaper. 'You shouldn't let yourself have ideas, Binkle.'

'Flip, listen!' cried Binkle, catching hold of him and sitting him down plump in his chair again. 'Wouldn't you like to have enough money to go on all the roundabouts and all the swings and see all the side-shows?'

'Yes, I would!' said Flip.

'Well, I'll tell you how we can,' began Binkle. 'You know how folk love to throw balls at things, in a fair, don't you? They love throwing at coconuts and things like that.'

'Yes,' said Flip.

'Well, Flip,' said Binkle, 'wouldn't it be lovely if we could somehow have Herbert Hedgehog to throw at? Think how exciting it would be to see if you could throw a ball and get it stuck on one of his prickles!'

'Binkle,' said Flip in horror, 'whatever will you think of next! As if Herbert would ever agree to that, anyhow!'

'No, he wouldn't *agree*,' said Binkle thoughtfully, 'but I might be able to think of some way that didn't need his consent.'

Well, after a few days, Binkle did think of a way, but he was so afraid Flip would refuse to help him that he decided not to tell everything.

'Look here, Flip,' he said, 'I just want you to take a letter to Herbert for me, will you?'

'All right,' said Flip, reaching for his cap. 'Let me read the letter first, Binkle.'

Binkle read it out loud.

'Dear Herbert Hedgehog,
'As you are one of the most important people of Oak Tree Town, we should be very much obliged if you would come and open our fair for us tomorrow at three o'clock sharp!'

'But I don't see the sense of writing a letter like that!' said Flip in astonishment.

'You wait and see!' grinned Binkle. 'That will be sure to bring Herbert to the fair all dressed up in his best, and with his new gold watch and all!'

'Still, I don't see how we –' began Flip; but Binkle sent him scurrying off, telling him to be sure no one saw him putting the letter into Herbert's letter-box.

Well, when Herbert got that letter, wasn't he pleased and proud!

'Oho!' he said to himself, standing all his prickles on end. 'So the fair people want me to open their show for them, do they? What will all Oak Tree Town say to *that?* I must dress up in my very best!'

He did. And very grand he looked. Last of all he put on his lovely new gold watch and chain. Then he looked at himself in the glass and was very pleased indeed with his appearance.

He set off for the fair, wishing that he could meet Sammy Squirrel or Dilly Duck, so that he might see their faces when he told them he was to open the fair.

But all he met were Flip and Binkle Bunny, also on their way to the fair.

'My!' said Binkle, when he caught sight of Herbert. 'My, Herbert! I never saw you so grand before. How fine you look!'

'I'm going to open the fair,' said Herbert importantly, swelling himself out proudly.

'Well, well, well!' said Binkle, holding up his paws, pretending to be most astonished. 'They made a good choice when they asked you, Herbert. I don't know anybody who could do it better.'

Herbert felt very pleased. He began to think Binkle wasn't such a bad fellow after all.

'Come along with me and hear my opening speech,' he said.

'We'd love to,' said Binkle, 'wouldn't we, Flip?'

'Yes,' agreed Flip, who was very much wondering what would happen when Herbert discovered he wasn't going to open the fair after all!

'But you know, Herbert,' said Binkle solemnly, 'you shouldn't have dressed yourself up so grandly, and you ccrtainly should-n't have put on your gold watch.'

'Why not?' asked Herbert in alarm.

'Well, there is sometimes a rough group of people at the fair,' said Binkle gravely, 'and if they see you dressed up like that, they might think you'd a lot of money on you – and *rob* you!'

'Oh dear!' said Herbert nervously. 'And I've got my new watch on, too. I wish I hadn't come. I think I'll go home.'

'Oh no, don't do that,' cried Binkle, catching hold of his arm. 'If you like, Herbert, Flip and I will stay with you and look after you.'

'Oh, *thank* you!' cried Herbert, thinking that Flip and Binkle were certainly two very nice fellows. 'That will be fine. Well, here we are at the fair.'

They went through the gates, and Herbert stared in astonishment.

'The fair's begun,' he cried. 'Surely I'm not late!'

'We must be,' said Binkle. 'Oh, what a pity, Herbert! Now you can't open the fair.'

Herbert was terribly disappointed.

'I'm going to see the head man about it,' he snorted. 'He's no business to ask me to come, and then to open the fair without me.'

But the head man was very rude. He laughed at Herbert, and said he was mad. Then he became angry and told Herbert to go away, or he'd put him into a coconut shy.

Binkle and Flip pulled him away.

'Never mind,' said Binkle. 'And don't say any more, for goodness' sake, Herbert. Else you really will be put into a coconut shy. Some people can be very rough, you know! And, oh dear! It is a pity you came all dressed up like this! I'm so afraid you'll be robbed.'

Herbert clung to Binkle and begged him not to leave him.

'No, I won't,' promised Binkle. 'Come and look round, Herbert.'

He took Herbert by the arm and led him off. Then Binkle did a very strange thing. He frowned and looked crossly at every single person he met. And, of course, *they* frowned back.

Presently Herbert noticed how crossly everyone looked at them.

'Why does everybody frown at us?' he asked in surprise.

'I'm afraid, I'm very much afraid they don't like you,' said Binkle. 'I expect the head man has sent the word round that you are not a nice person.'

Herbert began to shiver with fright. Just then three badgers and two stoats passed by and frowned most fiercely. He shivered even more.

'Here, Flip,' said Binkle suddenly, just look after Herbert for a minute. I'm going to talk to those fellows who've just passed us, and find out what's the matter with them!'

He left Herbert and Flip and ran up to the badgers and stoats.

'Hey, you fellows!' he said. 'Would you like to go in for a fine new throwing game?'

'What sort?' asked the badger.

'Well, you see old Herbert Hedgehog there,' said Binkle. 'I believe I can get him to sit down and let you throw potatoes at him to see if you can get them stuck on his prickles!'

The badgers grinned.

'Never heard of that before,' said one. 'How much does he charge?'

'I'll go and ask him,' said Binkle, and ran back to Herbert.

'I asked them why they looked so angrily at us,' he said to Herbert, 'and what do you think they said?'

'What?' asked Herbert and Flip.

'They said they'd never seen such an ugly fellow as you before, and the sight of your face was enough to make the fair a failure,' said Binkle untruthfully. 'I'm very much afraid you're in for a rough time, Herbert. You saw how everybody scowled at you, didn't you?'

Poor Herbert Hedgehog! He shivered and shook, and shook and shivered, and wished heartily that he'd never come to the fair at all.

'What shall I do?' he asked. 'I'd better go home.'

'I shouldn't do that,' said Binkle, 'it would look as if you were running away. No, I know a simpler plan than that.'

'What?' asked Herbert eagerly.

'I'll take you to a quiet seat I know over there,' said Binkle, pointing. 'There's a wall just behind it, and you can sit facing it, pretending to read a newspaper. Then your back will be to the passers-by, and no one will know who you are.

'They won't bother about my face if they can't see it,' said Herbert, with a sigh. 'All right, I'll do as you say.'

'Take him, Flip,' ordered Binkle, his wicked eyes dancing with delight and his nose going up and down with excitement.

Flip took Herbert off, and sat him down on the seat Binkle had pointed out, facing a wall. He gave him a newspaper, and then turned to see whatever Binkle was doing.

He was talking excitedly to a small crowd of badgers, stoats, and moles.

'Come on,' he said. 'You can have six throws for fifty pence. There he is, sitting over there, waiting for you to throw at him.'

'Ha! ha!' chuckled Miner Mole, polishing his spectacles. 'I'd like a good old throw at Herbert. He told me my cabbages were good for caterpillars but not for anything else, the other day.'

'And he said my beetroots would pass very well as radishes,' grinned a badger. 'Come on, boys, let's have a shot at him! What luck!'

A small crowd moved towards Herbert. Binkle produced a big basket full of potatoes which he had dug up from his garden that morning and hidden behind a tent, for he had no money to buy balls. From the basket he took a big notice, and balanced it upright against Herbert's seat.

SIX THROWS FIFTY PENCE!
SPIKE A POTATO ON HERBERT!

Then he started the game by throwing a few potatoes at Herbert himself.

Well, the coins began to roll in like anything. Directly Flip saw what was happening, he began giggling, but Binkle stopped him.

'Be quiet, Flip!' he whispered fiercely. 'You've got to keep Herbert still and pick up the potatoes. Pretend you're throwing them back! You can throw them to me and I'll put them in the basket.'

WHIZZ! WHIZZ! WHIZZ!

The potatoes began spinning through the air, and Herbert gave a tremendous yell of fright and almost fell off his seat.

'It's all right! Keep still!' said Flip. 'Your prickles will protect you, Herbert. I'll pick up the potatoes and throw them back, and keep the fellows off. Don't you worry!'

But Herbert *did* worry. He groaned, grunted, and yelled terrifically whenever a potato stuck on one of his prickles.

The crowd was delighted. Everyone thought Herbert was making a noise to amuse them, and more and more folk came up to join in the fun. The potatoes whizzed merrily through the air and stuck on Herbert, or burst into a score of pieces on the wall behind and spattered into poor Herbert's face. Flip picked up the whole ones and threw them back to Binkle as fast as he could.

'Don't you fret, Herbert,' he panted. 'I'm keeping them off all right.'

Soon half Oak Tree Town came to join in the fun. Dilly Duck and Sammy Squirrel and Brock Badger joined in, and laughed till tears ran from their eyes, to hear Herbert grunting and groaning.

Then Binkle caught sight of Wily Weasel, Oak Tree Town's policeman. At first he was frightened – then an idea came to him.

'Hello, Wily!' he called. 'Six for fifty pence! Have fifty pence worth?'

Now, Wily was a very good shot. He took six potatoes, stood back, and threw them quickly one after the other at Herbert.

Every single one stuck on Herbert's prickles.

But that was too much for Herbert. With a fierce howl of rage he swung himself off the seat, and faced Wily, who had just bought another six and was preparing to throw.

Herbert stared in amazement at Wily.

'Wily!' he gasped. 'Wily Weasel the Policeman! Why didn't you rescue me instead of joining these fellows? And Dilly! And Brock! and Sammy! How can you all stand by and see me treated like this! Gr-rrrrrf!'

He suddenly picked up a handful of potatoes and flung them hard at Wily and Sammy. Wily leapt across to Herbert and took hold of him angrily.

'Come on, Flip!' whispered Binkle. 'Now's the time for us to go!'

The two bad bunnies slipped away from the crowd.

Wily was trying to stop Herbert from throwing potatoes at everyone, when suddenly Herbert caught sight of the notice Binkle had put by his seat. He stared as if he couldn't believe his eyes.

'Oh! oh! oh!' he wailed suddenly. 'Six throws for fifty pence! It's all a trick – all a trick! Quick, Wily, catch Flip and Binkle.'

But Wily wouldn't till Herbert had explained everything.

Then he began to laugh.

'Oh, Herbert!' he cried, wiping his eyes. 'You'll be the death of me one day! You shouldn't be so silly! Fancy letting yourself be thrown at like that! You might have guessed Flip and Binkle were up to mischief.'

'Go and fetch them and scold them!' raged Herbert. 'Go on, Wily! They've got lots of fifty pences, all because of me.'

Well, in the end Wily did fetch them. He brought them to Herbert, who glared at them fiercely, and growled.

'Don't, Herbert!' begged Wily. 'You remind me of when you sat on that seat growling, whilst I threw six potatoes at you – and they all stuck!'

'Scold Flip and Binkle!' ordered Herbert. 'They've no business to make money out of me like that!'

Now, Binkle hated being scolded. An idea came to him.

'I'll give you half the money, Herbert,' he said, 'if you'll let us off being scolded. We've got a whole bagful.'

Herbert's little eyes shone. He loved money.

'All right,' he agreed at last. 'Give me half – but mind, you've been let off very easily!'

As Flip and Binkle went off to the roundabouts, Binkle chuckled.

'We *were* let off easily,' he said. 'We didn't deserve to be, either!'

And they certainly didn't – did they?

CHAPTER 6

Flip's New Job

Flip and Binkle Bunny were walking down Acorn Street when they came to the baker's shop. Derry Dormouse the baker was inside cooking, and a perfectly lovely smell came from the hot cakes he was baking.

Binkle stood still and sniffed.

'My,' he said, 'that smells, good! Got any money, Flip?'

'You know I haven't!' said Flip. 'I spent my last penny yesterday.'

'And I haven't any either,' said Binkle, sadly pressing his nose against the window and looking at all the lovely things inside.

'No one will give us a job,' wailed Flip, 'so I expect we shall starve! Oh dear!'

Suddenly Binkle caught sight of a little notice pinned up near the door. He went over to it and read it.

Then he scratched his head, leaned against the window, and thought hard.

'What is it, Binkle?' asked Flip, astonished to see his friend thinking so deeply.

'Sh! Wait a moment. I've got an idea,' said Binkle, beginning to look excited. 'Come and read this notice, Flip.'

Flip went up and looked at the notice. It was very short and neat.

> WANTED
> A quiet and clever nursemaid for four baby foxes. Please apply to
> Furry Fox
> Mossy Bank, Cuckoo Wood

'Well, I don't see anything in that notice to get excited about,' he said. 'We're not nursemaids! And I'm sure I wouldn't want to go and look after four sly little fox babies, even if I *was* a nurse!'

'Oh, you never think of anything!' said Binkle. 'You haven't got any brains at all, Flip! Look here! What about dressing-up as a nursemaid and going to see if we can get the job?'

'Gracious, Binkle, are you mad?' gasped Flip, sitting down suddenly on Derry's doorstep.

'Furry Fox is fierce enough to *eat* us if she found us out in a trick like that!'

'But why *should* she find us out?' argued Binkle. 'I can borrow some of my sister's clothes, and one of us can easily dress up. Old Furry Fox and her husband Fatty are rich enough to pay good wages, and four silly little fox cubs would be easy enough to look after.'

'Well, *you* can do the dressing-up,' said Flip firmly, standing up again. 'I'm not going to have anything to do with such a foolish and dangerous idea.' And he walked off with his head in the air.

'Flip!' called Binkle, running after him. 'Don't be mean! Help me to dress up, then! Come on to Bess Bunny's house with me, and see if she'll lend us some clothes.'

Well, Flip didn't mind doing that, and he went off with Binkle to call on Bess Bunny, Binkle's sister, who lived in Bramble Dell just outside Oak Tree Town.

They knocked at the door. Blim-blam, blim-blam!

Bess opened it. She was a thin, rather worried-looking rabbit, and had a large family of children. She wasn't very pleased to see Binkle and Flip, for they had a bad name in Oak Tree Town.

'What do you want?' she asked, when they were inside. 'You don't generally come and see me unless you want something.'

'I've brought you a present!' said Binkle in a hurt tone, putting a little bunch of pretty berries down on the table. 'We picked these for you, knowing how much you liked flowers and bright berries, for your dinner table.'

Bess looked pleased.

'Well, thank you, I'm sure,' she said, putting them in water.

'That's a new dress you're wearing, isn't it?' asked Binkle, looking at it very admiringly.

'Yes, it is,' answered Bess. 'My old one was getting so shabby!'

'Oh, that reminds me, Bess,' said Binkle. 'Could you lend me your old dress for a little while? I'd take great care of it.'

'What in the world for?' said Bess, in astonishment. 'Are you going to a fancy-dress party?'

'Well, not exactly that,' said Binkle. 'Something in that line, though.'

Flip giggled. 'You won't get Bess to lend you her old frock to go to a fancy-dress party in,' he chuckled.

'Oh, *won't* he!' snapped Bess, turning round and glaring at Flip, whom she disliked. 'Well, you're wrong. I *will* lend it to him.'

She ran out of the room to fetch it.

'That was a very clever remark of yours,' whispered Binkle to Flip, who looked most astonished, for he hadn't meant to be clever at all.

Bess came back with her old spotty dress and a small red shawl.

'Here you are,' she said. 'It's quite neat and tidy. Oh, and here's the bonnet to go with it.'

'Oh, that's fine!' said Binkle gratefully. 'You are a dear, Bess. We'll take it straight away, now.'

Bess wrapped up the things for them, said goodbye, and saw them off. Binkle was tremendously pleased. He rushed off to his cottage on Bumble Bee Common at such a pace that Flip could hardly keep up with him.

But what a disappointment when he tried the things on! They didn't fit him at all! For Binkle was plump and round, and Bessie's clothes didn't meet anywhere on him! Her little bonnet on his large head looked perfectly ridiculous. He was terribly disappointed.

'Here, you try them on, Flip!' he said at last.

So Flip, who was small and rather thin, slipped on Bessie's spotty frock. It fitted him perfectly! Binkle draped the little red shawl over his shoulders and pinned it in front. Then he perched the bonnet on Flip's head – and my, he looked as like a nursemaid as you could wish!

'Flip, you look fine!' cried Binkle. 'Look at yourself in the mirror. You *must* go to Furry Fox and see if she'll take you as a nursemaid.'

Flip looked at himself.
Certainly no one would think he
was Bad Flip Bunny, well known
all over Oak Tree Town for the
naughty pranks he and Binkle
were always up to.

'You would make a splendid
nursemaid!' coaxed Binkle, who
didn't want his lovely new idea
to come to nothing.

Well, after a lot of argument,
Flip at last said he would try. So
Binkle marched him off to Mossy
Bank and watched him go inside
the gate and knock at the front
door.

Poor Flip was dreadfully
nervous. He didn't like the Fox
family, for it was said that old
Fatty Fox enjoyed a meal of
rabbit pie when he could get it.

Furry Fox opened the door.

'Excuse me,' said Flip, 'I saw
your notice about wanting a
nursemaid.'

'Oh, come in,' said Furry Fox.

Flip stepped inside. He saw four
small fox cubs sitting in a row by
the kitchen fire, all sucking dum-
mies and looking as good as gold.

'Have you looked after babies
before!' asked Furry.

'No, ma'am, but I think I
could,' answered Flip nervously.

'Huh, you don't sound as if you
know much about it!' sniffed

Furry Fox, scornfully. 'I don't
think you'll do.'

Just at that moment Fatty Fox
came in. He stopped short at the
sight of the little rabbit.

'Ha! A new nursemaid!' he
cried. 'She looks fine, Wife! I
hope you've employed her!'

Furry looked at him, and saw
by the look in his eyes that he
thought Flip might come in
useful for a pie. She smiled.

'Well, I think we'll try you for
a little!' she said to Flip. 'You can
stay with us until Christmas, at
any rate. That's just a fortnight.
And I'll pay you a pound a day.'

Flip was very pleased to hear
that. A pound a day seemed a
great deal. He would be quite
rich at the end of two weeks.

'Thank you, ma'am,' he said.

Furry Fox told him to look after the fox babies whilst she and her husband went out. So Flip settled down by the fire with the babies, and as soon as the two foxes had gone, he took his pipe out of a pocket and began to fill it.

'Hist!' whispered a voice from the window, making Flip jump nearly out of his skin. He turned round and saw Binkle peeping through.

'Don't light your pipe, you fool! That will give everything away! Nursemaids don't smoke!'

Flip put his pipe away hurriedly, and began to tell Binkle how he had got the job for a fortnight at a pound a day. Binkle was delighted.

'My word!' he chuckled. 'We'll have a fine time after Christmas, spending the money, won't we?'

'Yes, but I don't like the job much!' said Flip. 'Can't smoke, can't sleep when I want to, and can't wear my own clothes!'

'Oh never mind,' comforted Binkle. 'You'll get on perfectly all right.'

But that's just where he was wrong. Flip got on very badly.

To begin with, *he* didn't know how to amuse babies. He didn't even know how to carry them. They squealed whenever he picked them up. And they had sharp teeth too, as Flip found out one morning when he was trying his hardest to dress the biggest baby. She didn't want her bonnet put on, so she set her teeth into Flip's paw, and my, didn't he jump!

'Ow! You little nuisance!' he shouted loudly at her.

You should have heard her howl! Furry Fox came running in to see whatever the matter was, and gave Flip a scolding for daring to upset one of her precious babies.

'Well, I'm not going to be bitten,' grumbled Flip under his breath.

'You'll be bitten harder still soon!' thought Furry Fox, thinking of Christmas and rabbit pie.

Every night Furry gave Flip, a round shiny pound, and he put it away in his pocket, feeling very pleased indeed to hear them jingle away there. A whole week went by, and Flip had seven pounds. He thought how pleased Binkle would be when he told him how rich he was getting.

Then after a few days something dreadful happened. Flip went out for a walk with the fox babies well strapped into their pram – and he came back with only *three* babies!

Furry met him at the door and was just going to ask if any of the babies had been to sleep, when she saw one was missing.

'Where is Fluffy?' she cried. 'What have you done with Fluffy? Have you lost him?'

Flip looked down at the babies and saw there were only three.

'Oh my!' he cried, in dismay. 'There are only three! I don't know what's happened to Fluffy!'

Furry Fox flew into a dreadful rage and caught poor Flip by the ear.

'Tell me what you've done with Fluffy or I'll eat you!' she cried.

Flip dropped down on his knees.

'Please have mercy!' he sobbed. 'I don't know, really. He must have dropped out of the pram when I wasn't looking. I'm terribly sorry.'

'Fine nursemaid *you* are!' snorted Furry, catching hold of him by the wrist. 'Come along. You're going to take me exactly where you've been with the babies, and see if we can find poor little Fluffy. If we can't – well!' and she glared at Flip so fiercely that he shook all over and his ears went floppy.

Furry dragged him through the wood, but though they looked everywhere for Fluffy, they couldn't see any sign of him.

So, growling with anger, Furry Fox dragged Flip home again, saying that she would tell her husband, Fatty, all about it. When they got to Mossy Bank, the three babies were playing in the yard. Furry counted them, snorted, and took Flip indoors, to call Fatty.

But directly they got indoors, Furry pricked up her ears. She heard something squealing upstairs.

And there on his cot in the nursery lay Fluffy, squealing for Furry!

'Oh! I must have forgotten to

put him in the pram with the others!' said Flip suddenly. 'I left him behind by mistake. So if I only took three babies out, I could only bring three babies back, couldn't I, Mistress Fox?'

Furry glared at him.

'I don't believe you're a nursemaid at all!' she cried.

'Well, I'm *not,*' said Flip unexpectedly. 'And I'm tired of your silly babies, so there. I'm Flip Bunny and I'm going home!'

He turned to go – but Furry caught hold of him.

'Oho!' she said. 'So you've been playing a trick on us, have you? All right! We'll play one on *you!*' and catching him by the scruff of his neck, she dragged him into a little room nearby and shut the door on him. He heard the click of the key turning in the lock, and he ran to the window. Alas! it was barred.

'That *was* a silly idea of Binkle's to dress up as a nursemaid,' he said. 'Suppose Furry and Fatty decide to eat me! How *can* I get away?'

He stayed there all day, very lonely and miserable. But when night came, he heard a noise of stones being thrown against his window. He peeped out between the bars.

'Hist!' came Binkle's voice. 'I was behind a tree when Furry went through the wood this morning, holding you by your neck. What's the matter?'

Flip told him.

'You must get away as quickly as possible,' said Binkle.

'I can't,' said poor Flip. 'The door's locked and the window is barred.'

Binkle thought for a minute.

'I've got a plan,' he said at last. 'Listen. I will rescue you. I'll do it this way. Are you listening, Flip?'

'Yes, rather!' said Flip.

'You must tell Furry that you've had a letter from Santa Claus to say he's bringing the fox babies presents on Christmas Eve,' said Binkle. 'Say he'll drive up to the front door and jingle his bells for you to come down and get the presents. Then we'll race off together and you'll be safe!'

Flip agreed to the plan, although he didn't really believe it would be much good. Binkle wrote a letter, tied a stone round it, and threw it up to Flip. It said:

I will come on Christmas Eve and bring presents for the Fox Babies. Santa Claus.

Next morning, Furry came into Flip's room, but before she could say anything Flip pushed the letter into her hand.

'Look!' he said, pretending to be excited. 'I know Santa Claus, so I expect he'll bring some lovely presents! This letter came in at the window last night.'

Furry Fox thought it was rather wonderful. She went out of the room to show Fatty the letter. Presently she came back.

'You can stay here till Christmas,' she said, 'and get the presents from Santa Claus.' Then she went out again and banged the door and locked it.

'And on Christmas Day you think you'll have me for dinner!' said Flip, chuckling. 'But you won't.'

Two days went by, and then Christmas Eve came. The fox babies were very excited to think Santa Claus was coming. Fatty and Furry kept a watch out, too, but the night was much too dark for them to see anybody coming.

Binkle was creeping up through the darkness. When he came to Mossy Bank, he took some little bells out of his pocket and tied them on to the branch of a tree. The wind blew them, and they tinkled like sleigh-bells.

'Santa Claus! – Santa Claus!' cried the babies.

Then a deep voice came out of the darkness.

'I am here! Do not keep me waiting!'

Furry took Flip and pushed him out of the front door. He ran out, and bumped into Binkle. Then he twisted his skirts up out of the way of his legs and *ran* for his life through Cuckoo Wood with Binkle.

Furry and Fatty waited and waited. They heard the bells tinkling in the wind and thought that Santa Claus was still there, talking to Flip.

'What a lot of presents he must be giving!' whispered Furry.

But Fatty grew suspicious. At last he ran out into the darkness and called to Flip. But there was no answer! Flip was far away. Then Fatty's head bumped into the tinkling bells, and he knew it was all a trick.

How angry they all were!

'And he's got ten pounds of ours!' snarled Furry. 'And we haven't any Christmas dinner!'

For their Christmas dinner was away in Heather Cottage on Bumble Bee Common, dressing himself in his own old clothes and smoking his pipe.

And with the ten pounds Flip and Binkle bought a lovely Christmas dinner – and my, didn't they enjoy it!

'No more dressing-up for me!' sighed Flip, as he ate a large mince pie. '*It's* too dangerous. *I* don't want to be anybody's Christmas dinner, I can tell you. I was lucky to get off as well as I did.'

And I really think he *was,* don't you?

66

CHAPTER 7

Binkle Has the Doctor

'I'm going down to Oak Tree Town to buy a stamp, Flip,' said Binkle. 'Are you coming?'

'Yes,' said Flip, reaching for his cap, 'I'm ready.'

Off the two trotted over Bumble Bee Common, down Hazel Road into Oak Tree Town.

But when they got to the post office, it was shut!

'Shut!' said Binkle in amazement. 'Shut! At eleven o'clock in the morning too! Fine sort of postmistress Dilly Duck is!'

Just at that moment someone walked up to the post office door.

'Mind, please!' said a little voice. 'I want to go in.'

'But it's shut,' said Binkle, turning round and seeing Timothy Mouse. He was carrying a steaming basin covered with a cloth.

'Of course it's shut!' said Timothy. 'Dilly's very ill. I'm taking her some soup my mother's made. Doesn't it smell good!'

And he went inside the post office and shut the door.

No sooner had he gone than someone else came up, carrying a big pink jelly on a dish.

'Good morning, Mowdie Mole,' said Binkle politely. 'Are you taking that to Dilly Duck?'

'Yes, I am. She's ill,' answered Mowdie, going into the shop.

Binkle and Flip stared at each other and sighed.

'Jelly and soup!' said Flip sadly. 'We never have those, Binkle.'

'And here's some flowers and grapes!' sighed Binkle, seeing Herbert Hedgehog coming up the street with his arms full.

The two rabbits went slowly home.

'Isn't it a pity one of us can't be a *little* bit ill!' said Flip.

Binkle stopped suddenly.

'That's a great idea of yours,' he said. 'One of us *will* be ill.'

'We can't be,' said Flip. 'We're both as well as can be, Binkle. Don't be silly!'

'I'm *not* silly,' said Binkle. 'I'm thinking about our idea.'

'It isn't our idea, Binkle,' groaned Flip. 'I don't have ideas. They're dangerous!'

But it was no use. Binkle was already making plans.

'Now shall you be ill, or shall I?' he wondered.

'*I'm* not going to be,' said Flip firmly, 'and I won't help *you* to be either, Binkle, and I mean that!'

'Fiddlesticks!' said Binkle rudely. 'You'll do just as I tell you, Flip. But you needn't be the ill one. I will, I should love that.'

'Oh dear! Very well, *be* ill!' said Flip desperately, and they went into Heather Cottage.

'I won't be ill *just* yet,' Binkle said – 'not till Dilly's better, anyway. People can't take broth and jelly to two people at once. I'll wait for a bit and think about it.'

He waited for a week and then heard that Dilly was up and about again.

'Now's the time!' he said.

He undressed and got into bed. Flip put a clean bed cover on, and made the room look as tidy as possible.

'Oh! Oh! Oh!' groaned Binkle in bed, rolling his eyes and opening and shutting his mouth.

'What's the matter?' asked Flip, in alarm.

'Nothing! I'm only just seeing if I can be ill properly,' grinned Binkle, tying a piece of red flannel round his neck. 'Now, Flip, you must do your part.'

'Part? What part?' asked Flip, his nose going up and down nervously. 'I'm not doing anything this time, Binkle.'

'Oh yes, you are,' said Binkle firmly. 'You're going to go to Sammy Squirrel the chemist, and ask him what's the best thing for a Shivering Fever.'

'Shivering Fever! I never heard of *that*!' said Flip.

'Nor have I,' chuckled Binkle. 'He'll ask you all about it, and you can say what you like. Say I've got headaches and a cold, and I'm hot and I'm shivering and I can't sleep!'

'Oh, Binkle, you're perfectly awful!' sighed poor Flip, putting on his coat. He went off, shaking his head, and wishing that Binkle wouldn't always be wanting to behave so badly.

He went to Sammy Squirrel's. There were a lot of people in the shop, but at last he got his turn.

'What's the best thing for a Shivering Fever?' he asked Sammy.

'Shivering Fever!' exclaimed Sammy. 'What's that? Who's got it?'

'Binkle has!' explained Flip. 'He's cold and he's hot and he's got headaches.'

'Headaches! How many headaches has he got?' enquired Sammy with a grin.

'He's got two,' answered Flip sharply. 'One at the front and one at the back.'

'I'm sorry to hear that,' said kind Dilly Duck. 'I've just been ill myself, so I know how horrid it is. After you've got the medicine

you want from Sammy, come in to me, next door, Flip, and I'll give you a jelly to take to Binkle.'

Sammy gave Flip a bottle of medicine to be taken three times a day. Then Flip ran in to the post office and Dilly gave him a red jelly in a big mould.

'Come and tell me how he is tomorrow,' she said. 'Has he had the doctor?'

'Er – no,' answered Flip. 'He says he won't see the doctor.'

'Dear, dear, dear, what a pity!' said Dilly, and when Flip had gone she went into Sammy's shop again and told him that Binkle wouldn't see a doctor.

'He may get terribly ill,' she said.

'Don't you worry, Dilly,'

grinned Sammy. 'Binkle isn't ill, he's only pretending. Why, I saw him yesterday looking as well as ever I've seen him!'

'But, Sammy, supposing he *is* ill,' said Gillie Guinea-pig. 'It would be horrid not to be nice to him, even if he is always up to tricks, and behaves so badly.'

'Yes, he's a bad bunny, but if he's ill we *ought* to be nice to him – I quite agree with Gillie,' said Mowdie Mole.

Sammy thought for a minute, then his eyes twinkled.

'I'll find out for you!' he promised. 'I'll pretend I'm a doctor, and I'll go and find out. If he is really ill, we'll do our best to be kind. If he isn't – well, we'll see!'

Flip would have felt rather uncomfortable if he had known what Sammy was planning. But he didn't know – so he went on towards Heather Cottage, carrying the jelly carefully, and occasionally giving it a lick, just to see if it tasted good.

'Well?' said Binkle, when Flip came into the bedroom. 'What has happened?'

'*This* happened!' said Flip proudly, holding up the jelly. 'It's lovely! I've licked it, to see!'

The two rabbits soon finished

up the jelly between them, and Flip told Binkle all that had happened. Binkle was very pleased.

'I expect lots of people will come and bring nice things,' he said hopefully. 'Do I look nice, Flip?'

'You look all right,' said Flip. 'What you've got to do isn't to look *nice*, though – you've got to look *ill*!'

Nobody else called that day, and Binkle was rather disappointed.

But the next day there came a terrific rat-tat-tat on the door.

'There's somebody,' chuckled Binkle. 'Go and see who it is, Flip.'

Flip opened the door. It was someone dressed in a smart suit and coat, and a black hat. In his paw he carried a bag.

Flip stared at him in surprise.

'I'm Doctor Curemquick,' smiled the visitor. 'Sammy Squirrel told me to come and look you up. Someone's very ill here, isn't he?'

Poor Flip didn't know what in the world to say!

'Well, Binkle isn't very well,' he stammered at last. 'He's upstairs in bed.'

'I'll go up and see him,' said the doctor, and pushing past Flip, he ran upstairs.

He walked into the bedroom and went across to the bed. Binkle stared at him in astonishment.

'It's the doctor, Binkle,' said Flip, who had followed close behind the visitor.

'I didn't ask any doctor to come and see me,' growled Binkle, twitching his ears nervously.

'No, Sammy Squirrel asked me to come,' said the doctor cheerfully. 'Now then, let's have a look at you! Put out your tongue!'

Binkle put out a very pink little tongue. The doctor looked at it and shook his head.

'Dear me!' he said, taking out a little note-book and writing something. 'Dear Me!'

'What's the matter?' asked Binkle in alarm.

'Now take a deep breath,' said the doctor, without answering Binkle's question.

Binkle took a deep breath and the doctor tapped him hard on the chest.

'Don't do that!' said Binkle. 'You hurt me.'

'Now flap your ears up and down,' ordered the doctor, writing busily again.

Binkle did so, feeling very nervous indeed at the sight of the doctor's grave face. He began to be afraid there really must be something terribly wrong with him.

'Dear me – dear me!' said the doctor. 'A very sad case – a – very – sad – case!'

'What's the matter with him?' asked Flip miserably, terribly upset to hear Binkle was really ill.

'Fiddle-faddlitis!' answered the doctor. 'I'll send him some medicine and some pills, and something to rub his chest with. He mustn't get up and he mustn't read. He must just lie quietly in bed and do nothing.'

'What shall I give him to eat?' asked Flip. 'Jellies and things?'

'Good gracious me, no!' said the doctor. 'Jellies and soups and things like that would kill him, in his state of health. Feed him on carrot-tops mashed fine, and nothing else. I'll call again in a few days.'

He ran downstairs and out of the house. All the way over Bumble Bee Common he chuckled and chortled to himself.

'I knew he was shamming,' he said. 'This will teach him to pretend to be ill. My, what a tale to tell the others!'

And when Oak Tree Town heard how Sammy Squirrel had dressed up as a doctor and gone to see Binkle, you should have seen them smile!

But Binkle and Flip weren't smiling.

'No jellies! No soups! No broths! What's the *good* of being ill?' groaned Binkle. 'Carrot-tops minced fine! Ugh!'

'Yes, this is what comes of pretending to be ill!' scolded Flip. 'If you hadn't pretended, you wouldn't really be!'

'Don't be silly!' said Binkle, feeling that he was showing very little sympathy. 'I feel very bad, so there! Oh! Oh! Oh!'

'Don't, Binkle!' begged Flip, who was really very upset to hear Binkle was ill. 'I can't bear it. I'll do all I can for you, you know that. I'll go and get some carrot-tops this very minute.'

But before he could do that, all the medicine came. Such an array there was! Boxes and bottles and jars!

Binkle tried them all. He was really afraid something was the matter with him, and he felt he ought to do all that the doctor had said.

But ugh, the medicine tasted dreadful! The pills tasted worse! And as for the stuff to rub on his chest – well, it smelt terrible!

Poor Binkle groaned and sighed, ate his carrot-tops and took his medicines. He didn't dare to get up, but just lay still in his bed as the doctor had ordered, feeling duller and duller each day.

Days passed, and no doctor came. Binkle had finished all the medicine and pills, and felt as if he never wanted to see a bottle again in his life.

'What's that doctor doing?' he groaned. 'Flip, go down to Sammy Squirrel's and ask him when Doctor Curemquick's coming again.'

Flip went – but, to his great astonishment, Sammy didn't seem to know anything about the doctor.

'Doctor Curemquick? Who *is* he?' he asked. 'He's never been heard of in Oak Tree Town before!'

'Well, you didn't send him, then?' gasped Flip. 'What an extraordinary thing! And poor old Binkle's been taking his medicine and pills every day, and they were as nasty as could be!'

'Has he finished them?' asked Sammy Squirrel, chuckling loudly.

'Yes, every one,' said Flip. 'What are you laughing at, Sammy?'

'Oh, just thoughts,' answered Sammy, chuckling still more loudly. 'Just my thoughts, Flip. They're rather funny!'

Flip's nose went up and down angrily.

'I believe you know more about Doctor Curemquick than you want to tell me!' he said, and stalked out of the shop and back to Bumble Bee Common.

He told Binkle that Sammy seemed to know nothing about the doctor.

'And Sammy seemed to think you being ill and having to drink medicine was a tremendous joke,' he ended.

'Oh! *Oh!* OH!' yelled Binkle, suddenly jumping out of bed with a tremendous leap. 'Well, of course it was a joke! A joke! Oh, my goodness! It must have been Sammy who dressed up as the doctor. I thought his face seemed a bit familiar!'

Flip's eyes opened wide.

'And he sent you all that nasty medicine – and made you stay in bed – and said you weren't to have jellies and soups!' he said. Then he suddenly began to laugh.

'It's – it's – it's very f-f-funny, Binkle,' he said, between his gurgles of laughter. 'You pretended to be ill – and Sammy pretended you were ill – and you thought you were and you weren't! Oh my!'

And he went off into peals of laughter again.

'Be quiet, Flip,' growled Binkle, beginning to dress himself. 'It isn't at all funny. It's a very horrid trick. It's very wrong of Sammy to pretend like that.'

'But *you* began it first,' went on Flip, chuckling loudly.

'Well, I shan't pretend any more,' roared Binkle. 'And if you don't stop laughing, I won't talk to you, so there!'

But though Flip stopped laughing, Oak Tree Town didn't.

And you can't think how red Binkle got when anyone he met asked him if he was *really* better!

CHAPTER 8

Binkle's Wonderful Picture

Binkle woke up one morning and tried to remember a dream he had had. He stared up at the ceiling and thought. It had been a very nice dream – he had done something that everyone admired – now, what was it?

'I know!' he cried suddenly, banging the bedclothes. 'I painted a wonderful picture!'

'Binkle,' shouted Flip angrily, waking up with a jump, 'stop hitting me!'

'You shouldn't be so near me, then,' said Binkle. 'Listen, Flip, to my wonderful dream. I dreamed I painted a marvellous picture of Oak Tree Town, and I dreamed that Rombo, the famous painter-rabbit came and told me it was the best picture he had ever seen. Fancy that!'

'What was the picture like?' asked Flip, very interested.

'That's the funny part,' said Binkle, frowning. 'However much I looked at it, I couldn't seem to see any picture at all. But everybody else did.'

'H'm – rather a silly dream,' said Flip, suddenly feeling sleepy again, and began to snore before Binkle could tell him any more.

But Binkle went on thinking about it, until, half awake and half

76

asleep, he found himself smiling over an absurd idea that had just occurred to him. He gave a chuckle.

'I'll do it,' he said, 'and see what happens.'

He went on planning until he had everything clear in his mind. Then he woke Flip up and told him what he was going to do.

'Don't be silly, Binkle!' said Flip. 'You must be half asleep to think of a thing like that.'

'I'm very much awake, thank you,' said Binkle, and tweaked Flip's nose, so that he squealed in anger and sat up to pummel Binkle.

But Binkle was already out of bed. 'That's right, Flip,' he chuckled. 'I thought that would wake you up.'

The two rabbits dressed quickly and got their breakfast. Whilst they were having it, Binkle told Flip what he was to do that morning, and gave him a long list of things to buy.

'And mind you tell everyone I'm going to paint a wonderful picture,' he ended.

Off went Flip to buy paint-brushes, paints, canvas, an easel, and a palette. He bought them all, but wouldn't let them be wrapped up. He wanted

everyone to see them.

Carrying them all carefully, he went slowly down the street, meeting Herbert Hedgehog, Dilly Duck, Derry Dormouse, and Riggles Rat, and many others who were doing their morning shopping.

'Goodness gracious!' they all cried, as one by one they met him. 'What in the world are you going to do, Flip Bunny?'

'I'm just taking these home to Binkle,' Flip told everyone. 'He's got an idea for a wonderful picture. Oak Tree Town will be proud of it, I can tell you!'

'Fiddlesticks!' grunted Herbert Hedgehog. 'You can't make *me* believe Binkle can paint.'

'You don't know what Binkle can do,' answered Flip. 'You just wait and see his picture, Herbert.'

Well, of course, all Oak Tree Town was very interested in Binkle's new work. They didn't quite know what to think about it. Binkle was a surprising Bunny, and nobody ever knew what he would do next.

So everybody talked about his painting and wondered how it was getting on and whether anyone would be allowed to see it. Which was just what Binkle wanted them to do.

Binkle was very busy. He had found a nice sheltered spot in the garden, and here he had put up his easel and canvas. He had also brought out his little stool and all his brushes and paints. He mixed a little of each colour on his enormous palette and thought it looked very artistic indeed.

But he didn't put a single dab of paint on his canvas. That was left quite empty.

Then he sent Flip into the woods with a spade and told him to dig up any old roots he could see, and if anyone asked him what he wanted, to say that he was taking Blue Fuzzymuz, Red Rillobies, and Purple Pittitoos for Binkle to mix with his paints.

'But why?' asked Flip, most astonished.

'To make my picture magic!' answered Binkle, with a chuckle.

So off went Flip with a sack and dug up bluebell roots and violet roots.

Riggles Rat saw him doing it, and wanted to know why.

'I'm taking Blue Fuzzymuz, Red Rillobies, and Purple Pittitoos to Binkle,' answered Flip. 'He mixes them with his paints, you know, and they make his picture magic.'

'How?' asked Riggles, amazed.

'I don't quite know yet,' answered Flip truthfully, going on his way with the heavy sack. 'Tell you tomorrow, p'raps.'

Riggles was most curious. 'Come to tea with me tomorrow,' he cried, 'and tell me all about it.'

'Right!' said Flip and went off.

He told Binkle about his meeting with Riggles, and Binkle laughed till he cried.

'Go and put those old roots in the shed,' he said, 'and then come back and I'll tell you what to say to him.'

When Flip came back, Binkle took him to his easel in the garden.

'What do you see there!' he asked, pointing to the empty canvas.

'Nothing,' answered Flip, rather astonished.

'Well, listen,' said Binkle solemnly. 'I'm painting a picture there that only *clever* people can see. Stupid ones won't see anything at all. It's magic, you see. My dream gave me the idea. When the picture's finished, we'll let people in to see it at twenty pence a time!'

Flip stared at him. He wished he hadn't said he could see nothing. Then something in Binkle's smile made him ask a question.

'Binkle,' he said, 'are you *really* painting a picture?'

'No, not really,' chuckled Binkle. 'But I don't expect anyone will like to say so, in case we think they're stupid. We'll just see how many people we take in, Flip. But I'm going to get Rombo the painter-rabbit to say it's wonderful first.'

'Rombo! But he'd never come. And he'd say you hadn't painted a picture at all,' cried Flip.

'Not the real Rombo! I'm going to ask my cousin Rab the Bunny from Bracken Hill Town to dress up and pretend he's Rombo,' chuckled Binkle. 'I've written to ask him to come on Friday. What fun! You must be sure and tell Riggles that, when you go to tea with him tomorrow.'

So next day off went Flip, dressed in his best, to see Riggles the Rat. He found that Herbert Hedgehog was there too, and Mowdie Mole, all very eager to hear the latest news of Binkle's painting.

Flip, feeling thoroughly naughty, began to enjoy himself.

'Oh yes,' he said in answer to their questions. 'Binkle's picture is getting on finely. It's a picture of Oak Tree Town and he's putting *everybody* into it!'

'Is he *really*?' said Herbert, most interested, hoping that he was somewhere well in the front of the picture. 'But isn't there supposed to be something magic about this picture, Flip?'

'Rather!' said Flip. 'He's mixed all sorts of peculiar juices in with his paints – I believe his great-grandmother once told him the secret – and – isn't this strange? – only really clever people can see the picture! Stupid people can't see a thing – it just looks like empty canvas to them!'

Nobody spoke for a minute. They were too astonished and too busy wondering whether they would be able to see this extraordinary picture or not.

Flip went boldly on.

'And Rombo the famous painter-rabbit is coming to see it on Friday,' he said. 'Fancy that!'

'Dear, dear, dear!' said Mowdie Mole, quite breathless with surprise. 'I'd no idea Binkle could paint.'

Nobody could talk of anything else all tea-time but Binkle's wonderful picture. And when Flip went home, he felt quite certain that everyone in Oak Tree Town would know about it before night had fallen. And he was quite right. They did! Mowdie, Riggles, and Herbert saw to that.

Herbert was tremendously excited. He was longing to see the wonderful picture, and longing to know what Rombo said about it. He decided to go up to Binkle's cottage on Friday afternoon and see whether Rombo really had arrived. Riggles said he'd go with him, and Sammy Squirrel too.

So on Friday afternoon all three walked into Binkle's little white gate, and saw Binkle sitting in the garden.

'Good afternoon,' he said kindly. 'I'm so sorry I can't ask you to stay, but I'm expecting Flip to bring Rombo here any minute to see my picture. But do call again afterwards, if you like.'

Rather crossly the three went out again.

'Let's hide here by this tree and hear what Rombo says,' whispered Riggles.

So all three hid silently behind the oak tree that stood next to Binkle's garden. But Binkle was watching out of the corner of his eye and knew quite well they were there. He chuckled to himself.

Presently Flip came up the hill with another rabbit. He was dressed in a black velvet coat and had a long flowing tie and wore very big glasses. Behind both his big ears were stuck lots of paint-brushes.

'Oh, good afternoon, Rombo Rabbit,' said Binkle politely. 'It is very good of you to waste your time on me and my picture.'

'Not at all, not at all,' said the make-believe Rombo, who was quite enjoying his part, especially as Flip had promised him a glorious tea afterwards. 'Where is your picture?'

'Here,' said Binkle, leading the way to where his easel stood in the shelter of the bushes.

Rombo peered at it closely. Then he stepped back and looked at it. Then he gazed at it sideways, and finally he went behind it. He came out in front of it again at last, and shook Binkle warmly by the paw.

'Binkle,' he said, 'it's *wonderful!*'

Herbert, Riggles, and Sammy, hidden behind the tree, looked at each other and shook with excitement.

'Did you hear that?' whispered Herbert. 'Binkle's a clever chap!'

'Sh!' said Sammy. 'Rombo's talking again.'

'In fact,' went on Rombo, 'it's *more* than wonderful – it's magic! Magic! Binkle, did you know that?'

'I hoped it might be,' said Binkle modestly.

'Yes,' said Rombo, shaking Binkle by the other paw. 'Mark my words, Binkle Bunny, no stupid person will be able to see that picture of yours. It will only be visible to clever people. Ha! Ha! Now you'll be able to see who's clever and who isn't in Oak Tree Town! Ha! Ha!'

'Ha! Ha!' said Binkle.

'Ha, ha, *ha!*' roared Flip, who had been nearly bursting all the time.

The three hidden behind the oak tree didn't laugh. They were all wondering which of them would be clever enough to see Binkle's picture. Herbert felt *quite* sure he would.

'Better wait here till Rombo's gone,' he whispered. 'Then we'll go and see it.'

The three rascally bunnies were having a glorious tea, and chuckling over the thought of the hidden listeners by the oak tree.

'You did your part well,' said Binkle to Rab, 'but why in the world did you go behind the picture, Rab?'

'He, he! To laugh, of course!' said Rab, stuffing a whole lettuce into his mouth. 'I could see Sammy Squirrel's tail sticking out, and I nearly choked. Ha, ha!'

'Ha, ha!' chuckled Binkle.

'Ha, ha, *ha*!' squealed Flip, who was almost ill with laughing. He never could stop, once he really began.

At last Binkle sent Flip home with Rab. Then he sauntered out into the garden, pulling his lovely whiskers and twitching his big ears. He went to the front gate. Ah! there were Herbert, Riggles, and Sammy Squirrel coming along, all looking rather sheepish.

'May we see your picture now?' asked Herbert.

'Er – well, I was thinking of charging twenty-pence to see it,' said Binkle. 'But I'll let *you* in for nothing, Herbert. The others can see it afterwards if they like to pay twenty-pence.'

'We'll wait and see what Herbert says,' said Sammy cautiously.

So Herbert, feeling very honoured to be let in for nothing, followed Binkle to where his easel stood in the bushes.

When he got there, he stared at the canvas in the greatest dismay – for he couldn't see any picture on it at all!

'That means I'm very stupid!' he thought miserably. 'Dear, dear, dear, and Oak Tree Town has always thought me so clever! I must pretend I see a picture. It must be wonderful if Rombo admired it!'

'Well, what do you think of it?' asked Binkle. 'Do you think the sky is blue enough?'

'Er – er – yes, quite!' said Herbert, pretending to look very close. 'Oh yes, decidedly. Oh, it's a wonderful picture, Binkle – wonderful! I shouldn't have thought you could have done it!'

'Oh, it was quite easy,' said Binkle truthfully.

'Er – I'll go and tell Sammy and Riggles to come,' said Herbert, terrified that Binkle might ask him a question he couldn't answer. He hurried to the gate and beckoned to them.

'What's it like?' they asked. 'Is it worth twenty-pence?'

'Oh yes, yes!' said Herbert. 'It's marvellous! Wonderful! Extraordinary! You really must come and see it! It's got a lovely blue sky!'

Well, Sammy and Riggles each paid Binkle twenty-pence and went in. They couldn't believe their eyes when they saw an empty canvas!

'To think old Herbert's clever enough to see it, and I'm not!' thought Sammy Squirrel in great disgust. 'I'm not going to say I can't see it, anyway.'

And Riggles thought just the same, and they began to praise it mightily.

'Finest picture I ever saw,' said Riggles, 'and the blue sky is lovely.'

'Yes, I'm rather pleased with that myself,' said Binkle. 'What do you think of the picture, Sammy?'

Well, Sammy thought a whole lot of things, but he wasn't going to say them. He asked a question.

'Who's that on the left-hand side of the picture?' he asked, pretending to look at it very hard.

'That!' said Binkle in a tone of great surprise. 'Why, that's Herbert! Fancy you not recognising dear old Herbert!'

Herbert bristled all over with importance.

'*I* recognised myself,' he said most untruthfully, 'and it's a *very* good portrait, Binkle!'

'Oh, very!' said Riggles, wishing to goodness *he* could see it.

'Best portrait of the lot, I think,' said Binkle, 'though of course Sammy's very good, too. That's him balancing a nut on his nose. Look,' and he pointed to the right-hand side of the canvas.

How Sammy wished he could see it! It made him feel quite ill, and he thought he'd better go home before the others guessed his stupidity.

The other two said at once that they would go too, and after thanking Binkle very politely for letting them see his masterpiece, they went off down the hill, solemnly talking about Binkle's picture.

'The sky was wonderfully good,' said Herbert.

'It was wonderful,' agreed Riggles.

'But your portrait was lifelike,' said Sammy, determined to keep his end up.

Well, of course, everyone in Oak Tree Town wanted to know what Rombo had said and what the picture was like. All three said it was wonderful and well worth twenty-pence to go and see.

'Of course,' said Sammy, with a laugh, 'you won't all see it, you know! Stupid people can't see a thing! It's a magic sort of picture.'

Everyone was most anxious to go and look at Binkle's picture, and next day the twenty-pences began to pour in.

Dilly Duck came first, and could hardly believe her eyes when she saw nothing on the canvas.

'I always had a sort of feeling I was stupid, and now I know it,' she thought miserably. But aloud she said, 'Yes, yes, yes! A lovely

picture! The blue sky is exactly the right colour.'

'Everybody says that,' said Binkle modestly. 'And do you like the trees?'

Dilly looked closely at the canvas and wished heartily she could see what the trees looked like.

'They're *very* nice,' she said, and then suddenly she said she must go home in case anyone wanted stamps. She was afraid Binkle would ask her more questions she couldn't answer. She didn't want him to guess she couldn't see anything.

Mowdie Mole, Susie Squirrel, and Derry Dormouse came, but they didn't stay long. They all said the picture was marvellous, especially the blue sky, and Herbert's portrait, and then they hurried off for fear anyone guessed they were pretending.

Creeper Mouse wanted to know if he could bring his children and Bess Bunny asked if she could bring hers.

'Oh, of course,' answered Binkle, 'but it won't be any use, you know. Children won't be clever enough yet to see my picture. But do bring them!'

So all Bess Bunny's children and Creeper Mouse's family came, and it was just as Binkle had said.

'*I* can't see any pretty picture!' said little Bobbin Bunny.

'I can't see anything!' said wee Mixie Mouse, nearly crying with disappointment.

Of course Bess Bunny and Creeper Mouse couldn't bear to be thought as stupid as their children, so they both said they *loved* the picture and thought it the best they'd ever seen.

Very soon everyone in Oak Tree Town had paid twenty-pence to see Binkle's picture, and all of them, except the children, who really couldn't be expected to be clever enough, said they had seen it, and liked it.

Then Herbert got an idea. He wondered if Binkle would sell it to him. He thought he would love to have a picture with himself in, especially one that would tell him which of his visitors were clever and which were stupid. So he went up to Heather Cottage and asked Binkle.

'I don't want to *sell* it,' said Binkle. 'I've got a lot of money just now. But I'll give it to you in exchange for six of your biggest cabbages, Herbert Hedgehog.'

Now, Herbert was very proud of his cabbages and he nearly said no. But then he thought of the extraordinary magic of Binkle's picture and he said yes.

'I'll bring the cabbages tonight,' he said, and ran off.

That evening he gave Binkle his six finest cabbages, and received in return Binkle's famous 'picture'. He carried it proudly off and hung it up in the dining-room of his little yellow house.

Everybody was very envious. Whenever they went to call at Herbert's house, he let them have a look at it, and though nobody ever saw anything on the wall but an empty canvas, gradually getting dirty, none of them said anything but, 'Wonderful picture, Herbert! Wonderful! You're a lucky fellow to have it!'

Now, when Binkle and Flip had eaten all Herbert's cabbages they went to call on him. He was sitting in his cottage, and Dilly, Mowdie Mole, Riggles Rat, and Sammy Squirrel were at tea with him.

'Come in, come in,' called Herbert. 'Very pleased to see our famous artist!'

Binkle and Flip went in and sat down.

'There's your wonderful picture!' said Herbert, waving his pipe towards the wall.

Binkle looked – then he looked again – then he stared hard and rubbed his eyes.

'Herbert,' he said reproachfully, 'you've washed all my picture off the canvas! It's absolutely empty! Isn't it, Flip?'

'Quite,' said Flip. 'Oh, what a pity! Such a lovely picture too! Everybody said how blue the sky was! Oh, Herbert, how could you?'

Herbert looked as if he was going to have a fit. His little eyes grew red and his prickles stood up on end. He couldn't say a word, though he wanted to, terribly badly.

'I'm *surprised* at you, Herbert!' went on Binkle sadly. 'Why did you do it? Oh! I believe I know. You wanted to make people say there was still a picture there, when there wasn't, so that you could laugh up your sleeve at them for pretending, in case anyone thought them stupid! Oh, Herbert, I didn't think it of you! My beautiful picture! All gone! All washed off! Not a trace left!'

Binkle took out his handkerchief, covered his eyes with it, pretended to sob, and walked out of the cottage, followed in a great hurry by Flip, who knew he would have to giggle very soon if he saw Herbert's astonished and indignant face much longer.

As soon as they had gone, Herbert snatched down the picture, broke up the frame, and put the whole thing in the fire. He saw through Binkle's trick very well indeed, but he knew that everyone would pretend he had washed off the picture, for no one would want to own up to how stupid they really *had been* in saying Binkle's empty canvas was a lovely picture.

'No one's ever to *mention* that picture again!' exploded Herbert Hedgehog, bristling with rage.

No one ever did – except Binkle and Flip, and they *would* keep saying what a pity it was to have destroyed Binkle's lovely blue sky *and* Herbert Hedgehog's portrait.

'And who would have thought,' said Binkle to Flip that night – 'who *would* have thought that silly old pretend-picture could really show us how stupid everybody in Oak Tree Town was! All of them thought they were so clever, yet nobody was clever enough to see through my little trick! Dear, dear, Oak Tree Town isn't very good at telling the truth! But we *have* had some fun out of it!'

And they certainly had.

CHAPTER 9

Bing-Bong, the Paw-Reader

Flip and Binkle had been good for a week and three days, and Binkle was beginning to find things very dull.

'Oh!' he moaned. 'Can't we find a more exciting job than delivering medicine for Sammy Squirrel the chemist? I hate carrying baskets of bottles every day.'

Flip preferred to be good. He was afraid of Binkle's exciting ideas – they nearly always led to trouble.

'It's a *very nice* job,' he said anxiously. 'For goodness' sake don't give it up, Binkle.'

Binkle put on his cap and opened the door of their home, Heather Cottage.

'Come on!' he said crossly. 'I won't give up the job – not until we get a better one, anyway!'

The two rabbits ran across Bumble Bee Common on their way to Oak Tree Town. When they got there, Binkle saw a big notice pinned up outside Dilly Duck's at the post office. He crossed over to look at it. In big letters it said:

```
A GRAND BAZAAR WILL BE
HELD IN OAK TREE TOWN
```

Binkle stroked his fine whiskers and began thinking. 'Come on,' said Flip, pulling him next door into Sammy Squirrel's. 'Don't dream like that, Binkle. It's time we began work.'

But all that day Binkle went on thinking, and hardly said a single word to Flip. In the evening, when Sammy Squirrel paid him, Binkle gave Flip a dreadful shock.

'We shan't be here tomorrow,' he said, 'so I'm afraid you must get someone else to do the job.'

'Oh, Binkle!' cried Flip in dismay. 'Whatever do you mean?'

'Sh! I've got a lovely idea!' said Binkle, pulling Flip outside.

'Come on, and I'll talk to you about it.'

'I don't like your lovely ideas,' wailed Flip.

'You'll love this one,' said Binkle. 'Listen. Did you read that notice about the bazaar outside Dilly Duck's?'

'Yes,' said Flip. 'What about it?'

'Well, at that bazaar there's going to be Bing-Bong, who can read all your life in your paw,' said Binkle excitedly. 'He'll tell you what's going to happen to you in the future, too.'

'Bing-Bong! I never heard of him,' said Flip. 'Anyway, what's it to do with us?'

'Oh, Flip, *can't you guess? One of us will be Bing-Bong*, and read everyone's paws!' said Binkle excitedly.

'Binkle! How can you be so silly?' gasped Flip. 'You *know* we can't read paws!'

'Well, we don't need to, silly!' grinned Binkle. 'We know all about everyone in Oak Tree Town, don't we, and we can easily tell them all about themselves. They won't know us, for we'll be dressed up and they'll think we're wonderful!'

'But how can we tell them what will happen in the future?' asked Flip.

'We'll make it up!' said Binkle. 'Oh, Flip, what fun it will be!'

'Will it?' said Flip doubtfully. 'But look here, Binkle – you're to be Bing-Bong. I don't look a bit like a Bing-Bong person. You do, you're so fat and big, and you've got such lovely whiskers.'

Binkle twirled them proudly.

'Yes, I shall be Bing-Bong,' he said, 'and you can be my assistant. First I must write a note to Herbert Hedgehog, who's getting up the bazaar.'

He sat down and got pen and paper. Presently he showed a letter to Flip. This is what it said:

> *Bing-Bong Castle*
> *Dear Sir,*
> *I am Bing-Bong, the reader of paws. I am passing through Oak Tree Town on the day your bazaar is held. I will call there and read paws.*
> *Yours faithfully,*
> *Bing-Bong.*

'There!' said Binkle proudly. 'What do you think of that?'

Flip's nose went nervously up and down as he read the letter.

'I do hope it will be all right!' he sighed. 'You *do* have such extraordinary ideas, Binkle. I don't know how you think of them.'

The letter was sent, and when it reached Herbert Hedgehog he was most excited. He at once arranged to have a little room set apart in Oak Tree Town Hall for Bing-Bong to sit in and read paws.

'It *will* be grand,' he said, 'and my, won't lots of people come to the bazaar!'

Binkle and Flip were very busy making clothes to wear. Binkle wore a purple suit with a red cloak wound tightly round him. On his head he wore a pointed hat with red stars painted all over it. He looked very grand.

Flip was dressed in baggy trousers and a little black velvet coat. He didn't like them much, for he felt he looked rather silly.

At last the day came, and the two rogues set out over Bumble Bee Common.

'Now, remember!' said Binkle. 'Call me Your Highness, and bow before you speak, Flip. You take the money and keep it safe. Leave the rest to me.'

Flip wished he could leave *everything* to Binkle, and not go at all, but he didn't dare to say so.

'Oh my! There's Herbert Hedgehog waiting to greet us outside the town hall!' he whispered. 'Do you think he'll see through our disguise, and know it's us?'

'Of course not!' snapped Binkle, striding forward. Herbert Hedgehog bowed very low when he saw the red-cloaked visitor.

'This is His Royal Highness Bing-Bong!' stammered Flip nervously.

Herbert stood all his prickles up very straight and made way for the two rabbits to go in.

'Very good of you to come, Your Highness,' he said, and led the way to the little room at the back of the hall. 'I've made this room ready for you. We shall love to have our paws read by the wonderful Bing-Bong.' And he bowed again.

Binkle looked round when Herbert had gone out.

'I'll sit in that big chair,' he said. 'You stand by the door, Flip. Charge twenty-pence a time, remember.'

Very soon there came a timid little knock. Flip swung the door open. Outside stood Creeper Mouse.

'Please, I've come to have my paw read,' he said nervously, holding out twenty-pence.

'Your Highness! Someone to have his paw read!' called Flip, beginning to enjoy himself.

Binkle put on some big spectacles and glared at Creeper, who stood tremblingly looking at him. He knew Creeper very well, for he was the postman of Oak Tree Town.

'Come here,' commanded Binkle, 'and hold out your paw.'

Creeper put out his tiny little paw. Binkle stared and stared at it.

'Your paw tells me many things,' he said. 'It tells me that you have five brothers and sisters. You are married, and you –'

'Oh! Oh! Oh!' squeaked Creeper, lost in wonder. 'How clever you are! It's quite true. Does my paw really tell you that?'

'Of course it does,' answered Binkle. 'Don't interrupt. It tells me that you walk miles and miles every day, carrying a heavy bag.'

'Yes, yes, I do,' squeaked Creeper. 'What's in the bag?'

'Your paw will tell me,' said Binkle solemnly, bending closely over it. 'Let me see – yes, you carry letters. You are a postman.'

'Well, did you ever!' exclaimed the astonished mouse, swinging his tail about delightedly. 'Oh, Bing-Bong, please tell me what will happen in my future.'

Binkle looked at his paw again. 'You will go on a long journey, in a ship,' he said gravely. 'You will carry letters all your life. You will have twenty-nine children.'

'No, no!' shrieked Creeper in horror, snatching his paw away. 'Twenty-nine children! Why, how would I feed them all? Oh! Oh! Twenty-nine children!'

And he rushed out of the room before Binkle could say another word.

Flip began giggling, but Binkle told him to be quiet.

'Sh!' he said. 'Creeper will be telling all the others at the bazaar, and in a minute they'll all want to come and have their paws read. Listen! There's someone now, Flip.'

It was Herbert Hedgehog, holding out his twenty-pence and looking rather nervous.

'Creeper Mouse says you're wonderful, Your Highness,' he said to Binkle. 'Could you read my paw, please?'

Binkle looked at it solemnly.

'You live in a yellow cottage,' he said. 'You grow very fine cabbages.'

'So I do – so I do,' said Herbert, in the greatest astonishment.

'You have many friends,' went on Binkle, 'but the two who love you best are – '

'Who?' asked Herbert eagerly, wondering if they were Dilly Duck and Sammy Squirrel.

'They are – Flip and Binkle Bunny!' said Binkle, now thoroughly enjoying himself.

Flip's nose went up and down in delight, when he saw the astonishment on Herbert's face.

'My best friends!' echoed Herbert. 'Flip and Binkle Bunny! Well, well, well! I must be nicer to them in future.'

'I *should*,' said Binkle, twirling his whiskers very fast, to hide the smile on his face.

'Tell me some more,' begged Herbert. 'Tell me about the future.'

'Er – if you dig up your biggest cabbages, you *may* find a pot of gold underneath,' began Binkle.

'Fancy! Oh, my goodness! Oh, excuse me!' begged Herbert, almost stuttering with excitement. 'Pray excuse me! I *do* want to go home straight away and see if I can find that gold.'

'Oh no, don't do that,' shouted Binkle in alarm . . . but Herbert was gone.

'Bother!' said Binkle in dismay.

'What did you want to go and say such a silly thing for?' demanded Flip. 'You *know* there's no gold under his old cabbages.'

'Sh! There's someone else,' whispered Binkle, as a knock came at the door.

It was Wily Weasel the policeman! Flip almost fell backwards in fright.

'May I have my paw read?' asked Wily politely.

'Oh – er – yes!' stammered Flip, wishing to goodness he could run away.

Wily went up to Binkle and bowed. Binkle took hold of his paw and glared at it. He didn't like Wily Weasel, for Wily had often scolded him and locked him up for being naughty. 'Your paw does not tell me nice things,' he began. 'It tells me that you are always hunting people and being unkind to them.'

'I have to be,' said Wily Weasel cheerfully. 'I'm a policeman! There are lots of rogues about Oak Tree Town, and I have to punish them!'

Binkle decided to change the subject. 'You are married,' he said, 'and you love to smoke a pipe.'

'Quite right,' said Wily, in a pleased voice. 'Now tell me about the future. Shall I get rich?'

'*Never*!' said Binkle firmly. 'You'll get poorer and poorer. You'll lose your job. You'll be hunted away from Oak Tree Town. You'll be put in prison. You'll –'

'Ow!' yelled Wily in terror, as he listened to all the awful things Binkle was telling. 'Don't tell me any more! I don't want to hear anything else!'

He went hurriedly out of the room, groaning and sighing.

'Ooh, I *did* enjoy that,' said Binkle. 'That's made up for a good many scoldings I've had from Wily.'

Thick and fast came the knocks on the door, and Binkle was as busy as could be, telling everyone about themselves. As he knew all their pasts and made up their futures, he enjoyed himself thoroughly – till in walked someone he *didn't* know!

He was a badger. He held out his paw to Binkle and waited.

'Er – er – er –' began Binkle. 'You live far away from here.'

'No, I don't,' said the badger. 'I live in the next town.'

'That's what I meant,' cried Binkle. 'Er – er – you are married.'

'I'm not!' said the badger indignantly. 'You don't know what you're talking about! You're a fraud!'

Just at that moment there came a great hubbub outside the door and it burst open suddenly. Herbert Hedgehog came stamping in, followed by a whole crowd of others.

'I've pulled up all the lovely cabbages in my garden,' he wailed, 'and there's not a piece of gold anywhere! And all my beautiful cabbages are wasted! You're a fraud, Bing-Bong – that's what you are!'

'Yes, he is,' cried the badger. 'Why, he told me I was married, and I'm not!'

Wily Weasel strode up to Bing-Bong and glared at him.

'Are you Bing-Bong, or aren't you?' he demanded. 'We're all those awful things true that you said were going to happen to me – or not?'

'Oh! Oh!' wept Flip. 'They weren't true, Wily, he made them up, truly he did!'

Wily turned round and looked at Flip and grabbed off his peculiarly-shaped hat.

'Oho!' he said. 'So it's Flip Bunny, is it? And I suppose Bing-Bong is our own friend Binkle?'

Binkle decided to make the best of it.

'Yes,' he said, 'I'm Binkle. I only came to the bazaar to give you a bit of fun. I'm sorry about your cabbages, Herbert. Flip, give him the money you've got. He can buy some more.'

Everyone stared in astonishment at the red-cloaked rabbit. They could hardly believe it was Binkle who had read their paws. They had so believed in him. For a minute everyone felt angry and probably Flip and Binkle would have got into trouble – if Creeper Mouse hadn't begun to laugh.

'He told me I'd have twenty-nine children,' he squeaked. 'Oh dear! Oh dear, and I believed him!'

Then everyone began laughing, and even Wily Weasel joined in.

'I'll let you off *this* time,' he said to Binkle. 'But next time – you just look out! Go off home, both of you. Give Herbert your money to buy more cabbages – and don't let me hear any more of you for a long time!'

Flip and Binkle scampered off to Heather Cottage as fast as they could go, very thankful to get off so easily.

And for two weeks Binkle had no more lovely ideas. After that – well you'll see!

CHAPTER 10

Binkle and Flip Try to Be Good

Binkle had got into trouble so often that he was beginning to be rather tired of it. He was seriously thinking of turning over a new leaf and trying to be good for a change. But he very much wondered what Flip would say.

He decided to tell him that night as they were getting ready for bed.

'Flip,' he said solemnly, 'what about being good for the rest of our lives?'

Flip brushed the hair on his big ears and sniffed scornfully.

'Don't try to be funny,' he said.

'But I mean it,' said Binkle, rather cross with Flip's sniff.

Flip stopped brushing and stared at Binkle in surprise.

'But you *couldn't* be good, Binkle!' he said, at last.

'I jolly well could, then!' cried Binkle indignantly. 'I tell you I'm tired of being naughty, and playing tricks on people. I'd like to be good and kind to them for a change. I'd like to go and visit poor old Mowdie Mole, who's got a cold, and I'd like to take Dilly some of our flowers, and –'

'And go and dig up all Herbert Hedgehog's garden for him, and wash up Wily Weasel's breakfast things?' suggested Flip, giggling.

'Oh well, if you're going to be *funny*,' said Binkle offended, 'I won't say any more. But you just wait till tomorrow morning.'

Flip thought he would. He couldn't understand Binkle's fit of goodness, and he wondered if he had eaten too many carrot-tops at supper. He rather hoped Binkle *would* still feel the same in the morning, because Flip, too, was getting rather tired of being naughty. He was really a harmless little bunny, who much preferred the quietness of being good to the excitement of being naughty.

Binkle might probably have woken up in his usual energetic, don't-care spirits if he hadn't had an awful dream. He woke Flip to tell him about it.

'Listen, Flip,' he said. 'I dreamed I went to Bess Bunny and played a trick on her. I dreamed I took Bobbin Bunny and Bimbo Bunny, her twins, and left two big turnips wrapped up in their cradle instead, to give her a fright. Then I took Bobs and Bimbo home, and when I got home, what do you think?'

'What?' asked Flip.

'They'd both turned into little fox cubs!' said Binkle.

'Ow!' said Flip, who hated foxes, big and little.

'That's not the worst,' said Binkle. 'They began to grow and grow and *grow* in my arms till I dropped them – and they were full-grown foxes! And they said, "Binkle, you shall be punished for your badness," and one of them ate me up! Oh dear, dear!' And Binkle shivered at the thought.

Flip shivered too. 'What did the second fox do?' he asked.

'He ate *you* up,' answered Binkle solemnly.

'Ow!' said Flip again, and dis-appeared beneath the bedclothes. Binkle thought he would too, and together the poor bunnies trembled under the blankets.

'It shows we'd better be good,' whispered Binkle, after a time.

'Yes,' agreed Flip in a muffled voice. 'Take your ear out of my mouth, Binkle, and sit up and see if we're safe.'

Binkle began to feel better, and bravely sat up. The sun was streaming into the bedroom and he began to laugh.

'It's all right,' he said, 'let's get dressed. We'll go straight down to Mowdie Mole's and offer to read to her while she's in bed with her cold.'

So the two rabbits dressed quickly and went down to Mowdie Mole's. They knocked at the door and waited.

No answer.

They knocked again. Still no answer.

'Mowdie Mole,' called Binkle, 'we've come to read to you.'

Not a sound came back to them in answer.

'Dear, dear!' said Flip anxiously. 'Do you suppose she's too ill to answer us, Binkle?'

'I expect she is,' said Binkle. 'It's a mercy we came along. We can get her breakfast, perhaps. Won't that be a kind thing to do, Flip?'

'Yes,' agreed Flip, wondering if Mowdie Mole would let them share her breakfast.

'Look here,' said Binkle, 'that window's open up there. Let me stand on your back and I'll climb in. Then I'll open the door to you, Flip.'

In half a minute Binkle was inside Mowdie Mole's house, and let Flip in too. They went and listened outside Mowdie's door.

'I *think* I can hear her breathing,' said Binkle. 'She must be asleep. It would be a nice surprise for her if we got her breakfast ready without telling her, and took it up, wouldn't it?'

Flip thought it was a fine idea, and the two rabbits went to the kitchen. They found some milk and put it on the fire to boil, and Binkle thought he could make some nice soup of onions, carrots, and potatoes. So he got them all out and began cutting them up.

Suddenly they heard footsteps outside, and then the front door opened!

'Who *can* it be?' gasped Flip in fright.

They soon saw – for who should come walking straight into the kitchen but Mowdie Mole herself! She nearly fell down in astonishment when she saw Binkle and Flip cutting up onions and carrots in her kitchen.

'Binkle! Flip! What *are* you doing?' she demanded.

'We thought you were ill in bed!' said Binkle, feeling very small.

'Ill in bed!' snorted Mowdie Mole. 'You thought nothing of the sort! You knew I was out shopping, so you thought you'd come and help yourselves while I was gone. I didn't think you were quite as bad as t*hat*, Binkle Bunny!'

'We're *not*!' said Flip indignantly, finding his tongue, 'We really thought you had a cold and were ill in bed – so we're getting your breakfast to take up to you. We're trying to be good!'

'Trying to be good,' laughed Mowdie scornfully – 'when everybody *knows* you never have been! You want scolding, and I'm going to do it! The idea of messing up my nice kitchen like this!'

She pounced on Flip – when sizzle-sizzle – sizzle! The milk in the saucepan boiled over.

'Oh, my nice clean stove!' wailed Mowdie, and ran to take the saucepan off the fire.

Binkle and Flip took to their heels and ran out of Mowdie's kitchen like a streak of lightning. They didn't stop running till they were back at Heather Cottage.

Then they sat down and looked at each other.

'It's hard to be good and kind,' said Binkle sorrowfully.

'But we mustn't give up,' said Flip. 'You won't, will you, Binkle?'

'Not *just* yet,' agreed Binkle. 'We'll take Dilly Duck a big bunch of our best pink roses next, I think. She *will* be so pleased. Come and pick them, Flip.'

They picked two great bunches of roses, and, each carrying one, they walked down to Oak Tree Town, feeling very kind and generous. Just as they got to Herbert hedgehog's, Binkle stopped.

'Look!' he said to Flip, pointing to Herbert's side gate. 'Herbert's left it open. Let's go and shut it for him, Flip, in case any thieves get in.'

The two bunnies went into the front garden and slammed the side gate. Then they turned to go out again – and whom should they meet coming in but Herbert Hedgehog!

He stared at them in surprise.

'Good morning, dear Herbert,' said Binkle politely. 'We just saw your side gate open, and shut it for you.'

Herbert looked even more surprised.

'Stuff and nonsense!' he said rudely. 'Never heard of you shutting anyone's gate for them before. No, you've been picking my roses – that's what you've been doing, you pair of rascals!'

'We *haven't*!' said Binkle indignantly. 'We picked these out of our own garden!'

'And what did you mean to do with them?' asked Herbert disbelievingly.

'We're taking them to Dilly Duck as a little present,' said Flip.

'Taking them to – Oh, ha, ha, ha!' roared Herbert. 'Never heard of you giving anyone a present before, Binkle. Ha, ha, ha! And my roses, too!'

'They're *not* your roses,' stormed Binkle. 'Come on, Flip, let's go before this silly old hedgehog makes us angry.'

Herbert stopped laughing.

'If you go out of my gate, I'll call Wily Weasel,' he said. 'He's just over there, and I'll tell him how I saw you coming out of my side gate with bunches of roses to take to Dilly Duck. Do you think he'll believe you?'

Binkle thought Wily Weasel most certainly would *not* believe them, and he grew very angry.

'*Take* the roses, then,' he shouted, and banged the whole bunch down on Herbert Hedgehog's head. Flip did the same, and before the surprised hedgehog could call for help, the two bunnies dashed out of the garden and were far away up the road.

'*Well*!' choked Binkle in great disgust. 'That's the last time *I'll* ever try to be good! All our roses wasted!'

Flip mopped his hot nose with his big red handkerchief and smoothed back his floppy ears.

'Let's try just once more,' he begged. 'People say the third time's lucky, you know. And everybody says it's hard to be good, so it's no wonder we don't find it very easy, is it, Binkle?'

'Well, what's the use of being good if people only think we're being naughty?' demanded Binkle crossly. 'You can go on being as good as you like, Flip. I've *stopped*.'

Binkle sat down by the roadside and fanned himself. Flip sat down too, and tried to make Binkle change his mind.

But Binkle wouldn't. He pushed Flip away and settled himself comfortably to have a nap.

'Go and be good somewhere else,' he said. 'You're disturbing me.'

Flip wriggled his nervous little nose in despair. Then he looked down the road, for he heard footsteps.

It was Brock Badger carrying a large and heavy sack.

'Look, there's Brock Badger,' said Flip. 'He's got a sack. Let's go and help him, Binkle.'

Binkle snored hard.

'You'll hurt your throat if you do that,' said Flip 'I know you're not asleep. Come and help Brock, Binkle. He's limping.'

'Snore, snore!' went Binkle as loudly as ever he could.

'All right,' said Flip crossly. 'I'll go and be good by myself.'

He got up and went down the road to meet Brock Badger.

'Good morning,' he said. 'Is that sack heavy? You seem to be limping!'

'I've got a thorn in my foot,' said Brock.

'Well, let me carry your sack home for you,' offered Flip, in his kindest voice. 'Then your foot won't hurt so much.'

Brock stared at him in surprise.

'No thanks,' he said. 'I know your tricks, Flip. You'd run off with my sack, and I couldn't catch you with my bad foot.'

'I *wouldn't*,' cried Flip. 'I'm trying to help you.'

'Hm, that's a new idea,' said Brock disbelievingly.

'Perhaps you haven't heard,' explained Flip, 'Binkle and I are trying to be good now. At least, Binkle's a bit tired of it, but I'm not. Let me help you, Brock Badger.'

'All right,' said Brock, seeing that Flip really did mean what he said. 'Very kind of you, I'm sure. Catch hold.'

He gave the sack to Flip, and together they went up the road.

They passed Binkle, who was lying just where Flip had left him.

'Snore, snore!' he went, as they passed.

'Being good seems to have tired him out,' remarked Brock. 'I don't wonder. It must have been very difficult for anyone so dreadfully naughty as Binkle.'

Now, Binkle wasn't really asleep – only pretending – and he distinctly heard what Brock said to Flip. It annoyed him very much.

He opened one eye just as they had passed him. And he saw something that nearly made him sit up with delight.

The sack Flip was carrying was full of carrots. It had a hole at the bottom, and Binkle saw a long red carrot drop quietly out in the road.

In a second he jumped up. He ran into Heather Cottage, which was just near by, and picked up a sack of his own. Then he ran back to the road.

There lay the carrot! Flip and Brock weren't in sight, for they had turned a corner.

Binkle picked up the carrot and popped it into his sack. Further on lay another one, and he picked that up too, and ran on again to a third one.

When he came to the corner, he peeped round it. He could see Flip and Brock in the distance, plodding along not knowing anything about the hole in the sack. He waited till they had turned another corner, then on he went again, picking up the dropped carrots quickly and popping them into his sack with a chuckle.

'Carrots don't seem to stay long with good people' he laughed.

Flip and Brock were going along talking. At first Flip found the sack very heavy, but soon it seemed to feel lighter.

'I must be getting used to the weight,' he thought, and padded along happily, thinking how nice it was to be good.

Brock began to think Flip wasn't such a bad bunny after all.

'I'll give you six of my carrots when we get home,' he promised. 'It's very nice of you to carry my heavy sack.'

'Oh, it's not a bit heavy,' said Flip truthfully. Quite half the carrots had fallen out by this time, though neither Flip nor Brock knew it. Binkle was picking them all up, and his sack was not nearly so light as it was at first. He was very careful to keep well out of sight, for he had no intention of being caught.

At last Flip and Brock reached the Badger's house. Flip took the sack off his shoulders and put it on the ground. There seemed to be something the matter with it. It looked very thin and empty.

Flip and Brock both stared at it.

'*Where are my carrots?*' roared Brock suddenly, catching hold of Flip's collar.

'Don't, Brock!' cried Flip. 'Look, there's a hole in your sack! They must have tumbled out!'

'You did it on purpose, so that you could go back and pick them up,' shouted Brock, shaking Flip until his ears flapped his nose.

'I *didn't!*' he cried indignantly. 'Come back with me along the road and get them. They'll all be there, you'll see!'

So Brock and Flip went back to the road – and, to Flip's enormous astonishment, not a single carrot could he see, even though he went right back to where he started. He really couldn't understand it.

'Are you *sure* there were carrots in your sack?' he asked Brock.

Brock bristled all over with rage, and made a pounce at Flip and caught him by the fur of his neck.

'*Carrots!*' he snorted. 'Of course there were! Now I'm going to scold you, you wicked little rabbit!'

Flip gave one tremendous yell of fright, jerked himself away from Brock, and ran to Heather Cottage as fast as ever he could. Brock was left behind with a handful of fur and a bad temper.

Flip rushed into Heather Cottage and banged the door. He went into the kitchen and sat down, trembling, on a chair.

Binkle was there, and he looked rather surprised to see Flip come in in such a hurry.

But Flip was even more surprised than Binkle when he saw what was on the floor – for there stood a large sack of carrots!

He stared at them as if he couldn't believe his eyes.

'Oh-oh! There's Brock's carrots,' he groaned.

'No *my* carrots,' said Binkle. 'I found them. And finding's keeping.'

'It isn't, when you know the owner,' said Flip. 'If it hadn't been for you picking up the carrots that dropped out of the sack, I wouldn't have got a sore neck. Brock's pulled half my fur off.'

'Serves you right,' said Binkle. 'I told you you ought to have stopped trying to be good.'

This was too much for Flip. He jumped up in a fury, caught hold of Binkle's collar and jerked him to his feet.

'It's your naughtiness that made my kindness no use,' he stormed. 'Come on outside. I'm going to give you such a shaking that the dust will fly. Grr-rrr-rr!'

He ran Binkle outside into the garden and twisted his arm until it ached. Binkle struggled and fought and at last got free. He ran indoors.

'All right,' he said, 'I'll have all the carrots – see!'

But, oh, my goodness! No sooner had he got indoors than he stood and stared in fright. For Brock, who had been listening outside the window, had jumped in, got the sack of carrots, and jumped out again. He put his head in the window and made a face at Binkle.

'I shook Flip, and Flip shook you,' he grinned, 'so you've both had a good shaking, which is what you deserve! And I've got my carrots back, and a new sack. Thank you very much, Binkle Bunny.'

He ran round the garden and bumped into Flip. He took out a big carrot and gave it to him.

'Here you are,' he said. 'It wasn't your fault. Go and tell Binkle what you've got for being good.'

Off he went chuckling, with his sack on his back.

And when Binkle looked out of the window and saw Flip sitting down comfortably, eating a very large carrot, he was very annoyed indeed.

But Flip looked so terribly fierce that Binkle really didn't dare to ask him for even a bite. So he went to bed instead, which is the best place really for bad bunnies.

CHAPTER 11

Flip's Sunstroke

'Who's that coming up to the door?' asked Binkle, peering out of the window.

'He looks very scruffy,' said Flip. 'He's got something under his arm to sell.'

Rat-tat-tat! The door-knocker made a loud noise.

Binkle opened the door.

'Good morning,' said the visitor 'May I come in and show you my pictures? I'm Firky Fox, and I paint pictures with my brush. Beauties they are, too, I can tell you.'

Binkle didn't like foxes.

'No, you can't come in,' he said. 'Show me your pictures here.'

Firky held them out one by one.

'Oak Tree Town at Sunset,' he said. 'A very nice one, that. See the red sunshine on the windows! And here's Bracken Hill with the snow on it. A real beauty!'

Flip came and peeped over Binkle's shoulder.

'We don't want pictures, Binkle,' he said.

'Here's a nice one now!' said Firky. 'A field of turnips.'

'Yes, that is nice,' agreed Binkle, wishing it was real. 'I'll take that one. Yes, and I'll have this one too, with the cabbages and lettuces on a dish. And that one with all those hazel-nuts and acorns – and what about this one with the beetles and the cheese?'

'Oh Binkle!' gasped Flip in amazement. 'What in the world are you thinking of? You're not going to buy those pictures, surely!'

Binkle took no notice of Flip. He took out his purse, and counted out some money.

'There you are,' he said to Firky. 'I'll give you that for these four pictures.'

'Thank you,' said Firky, handing them over. 'They're cheap at the price!'

He packed the rest of the pictures under his arm, and went off, whistling cheerfully.

Binkle carried the four pictures indoors, set them on the floor against the wall, and looked at them. Flip looked as if he thought Binkle was quite mad, and he rubbed his nose nervously with his paw.

'Do you feel quite well, Binkle?' he asked.

Binkle laughed.

'Yes,' he answered. 'And I haven't bought these pictures to hang up. Oh no, Flip! I've got a better idea than that.'

Flip groaned. 'What is it?' he asked. 'I shouldn't think we've got a single penny left after you've paid Firky Fox.'

'We haven't!' said Binkle cheerfully. 'But we're going to make *lots* of money with the help of these pictures.'

'How?' asked Flip curiously.

'Like this!' laughed Binkle, and picked up a piece of white chalk. He knelt on the floor and wrote with it. Then he sat down by the pictures, looking thoroughly miserable, and held out his cap.

ALL MY OWN WORK
PLEASE SPARE A COIN TO KEEP
ME AND MY OLD FATHER

was what he had written on the floor.

'Oh!' gasped Flip. 'Binkle, you are dreadful! Whatever will you do next?'

'Any amount of things!' said Binkle, with a grin. 'First, I'm going to take these to Bracken Hill Town, where we're not well known. I'm going to find a nice sunny corner and sit down by my pictures. I shall have such a lovely lazy day, and only have to count how many coins come rolling in!'

'But what about your poor old father?' asked Flip. 'You haven't *got* a poor old father.'

'Oh yes, I have!' chuckled Binkle. 'You're the poor old father, Flip. I'm going to wrap you up in a shawl, and wheel you down to Bracken Hill Town in a wheelchair. You can go comfortably to sleep all day, if you like.'

Flip wriggled his nose and thought.

'All right,' he said at last. 'There doesn't seem to be much danger in your plan. I'll come.'

The two rascals began to make ready. Binkle fetched an old wheelchair out of the shed, and cleaned it up. Then he wrapped Flip in a big blue shawl, and put him in the chair. He placed the pictures on Flip's knees and started off.

Over Bumble Bee Common he went, pushing Flip along quickly. Bumpity-bump! went the chair over the bracken and heather, and shook all the breath out of Flip's body!

'Let me get out and walk!' he begged. 'I can't stand this!'

'You're not standing it, you're sitting it,' answered Binkle cheerfully, going faster than ever – so fast that poor Flip hadn't breath enough to say another word.

At last they arrived at Bracken Hill Town, and Binkle slowed down. He went down the village street, pushing Flip along, looking for a nice sunny corner.

'Here's one that will do,' he decided. 'It's sunny, and it's just near the market-place, so there'll be lots of people passing.'

He wheeled Flip to the side, and fixed the chair so that it wouldn't run down the pavement. Then he spread out his pictures, wrote on the pavement with chalk, sat down on a cushion he had brought, and held out his cap.

Binnie Badger came hurrying by from market, carrying a bag full of potatoes. She stopped and looked at the pictures.

'That picture of the beetles is very good,' she said. You're a

clever painter. Here's fifty pence for you,' and she put it into Binkle's cap.

'Thank you, ma'am,' said Binkle.

'Thank you, ma'am,' croaked Flip in a very quavery old voice.

Then came Susie Squirrel hurrying to market to buy nuts for dinner. When she saw the picture of nuts and acorns, she stopped with a squeak of delight

'I almost thought they were real,' she said. 'They're just what I'm going to buy for dinner. Here's something for you,' and she threw a coin into Binkle's cap.

'Thank you kindly, ma'am,' said Binkle.

'What did she give you?' asked Flip in a whisper.

'Twenty pence,' answered Binkle. 'Sh! There's a lot of folk coming now!'

Bibs Bunny thought the turnip-field picture was wonderful and she gave Binkle fifty pence. So did Bobtail Bunny, her husband. Hickory Hare loved the picture of the cabbages and lettuces, and Mary Mouse thought the cheese picture was beautiful.

Soon Binkle's cap was jingling with coins, and he could hardly stop himself whistling merrily.

'Fine supper we'll have tonight!' he whispered to Flip.

'I hope we *shall!*' said Flip. 'You've got the best of things, I can tell you. I'm getting hungry, and my! The sun is hot! Can't I take off this shawl, Binkle?'

'Good gracious, no!' said Binkle sharply. 'Everyone will see you're not an old rabbit, then. And don't stick your ears up straight like a youngster. Flop them down over your nose, as if you were tired out.'

Flip did so, and heaved a great sigh. Sally Stoat, who was just passing, felt very sorry for him.

'Poor old fellow!' she said. 'I'm sorry to see you're feeling ill. I'll give a pound to your son, and perhaps he can buy you some medicine to make you better.'

She dropped a pound into Binkle's cap and went on her way to market.

'A pound! That will buy you a fine lot of medicine, Flip!' chuckled Binkle.

'You just try buying me medicine!' scowled Flip. 'Buy me some lemonade instead. I'm thirsty enough to drink a bucketful.'

'That's a good idea of yours,' said Binkle. 'I'll leave you here for a minute and go and get you something to eat and drink.'

'Don't be long,' said Flip.

'No,' promised Binkle, and off he went down the street to look for a lemonade shop.

Flip began thinking of what Binkle might bring back. He thought happily for about ten minutes, then he began to wish Binkle would come back.

He craned his neck round to the left, and looked down the street, but he could see no signs of Binkle!

'Oh, dear!' he groaned. 'I did think he'd be quick. Ah! there's somebody! Perhaps it's Binkle!'

But it wasn't. It was Dinky Dormouse. She stopped opposite Flip's chair, and looked at him.

'So your son's gone and left you, has he?' she said. 'Well, I hope he'll come back. It isn't safe to leave an old fellow like you alone, in the road. Anything might happen.'

Flip began to feel alarmed.

'Whatever *has* happened to Binkle?' he thought anxiously. 'He said he wouldn't be long! And what can I do? I'm supposed to be an old rabbit, and can't walk. Folk would know we'd been playing a trick on them if I suddenly jumped out and went to look for Binkle. Oh, dear me!'

Still Binkle didn't come. Half an hour went by, and another half an hour!

Flip got more and more worried. He couldn't think what in the world to do. Folk stared at him in surprise, as they passed, and wondered why he was all alone. Flip couldn't bear it.

The sun got hotter and hotter, and he suddenly felt very sleepy. He struggled to keep his eyes open, but it was no good. They would keep shutting themselves – and in two minutes Flip was sound asleep, dreaming of lemonade and lettuces.

Presently Sally Stoat came back from market. She was very surprised to see that Flip was all alone.

'Where's your son gone?' she asked him.

Flip made no reply. He was dreaming hard.

'Where's your son gone?' asked Sally in a louder voice.

Flip went on sleeping.

Then Sally became alarmed, and bent over him. She saw his eyes were shut and she thought he must be ill.

'Poor old fellow!' she said. 'I think I'd better get help. Maybe he's got a sunstroke, sitting here in the sun!'

She beckoned to Dinky Dormouse, who was on her way back home.

'Dear, dear!' said Dinky in alarm. 'He was all alone when I passed, about half an hour ago. Hadn't we better do something?'

'Let's wheel him over to Hanna Hare's,' said Sally. 'Perhaps she'll know what to do for sunstroke.'

So together they unfixed the wheelchair and pushed it up the street to Hanna Hare's.

'Whoever have you got there?' asked Hanna in surprise.

'A poor old rabbit with sunstroke,' explained Dinky. 'His son has left him, and we're afraid the poor old thing is ill. What do you do for sunstroke, Hanna?'

'We must put ice on his head and put him in a dark room,' said Hanna anxiously. 'Dear, dear, what a sad thing! But first we must unwrap him and get him out of his chair.'

All this time Flip had been soundly sleeping, and not even when he was being wheeled away did he awake. But when Dinky began pulling at the shawl round his neck, he woke up with a jump.

'Ow!' he said. 'Stop it, Binkle.'

Then he caught sight of Dinky and Sally and Hanna.

'Ooh!' he said. 'Am I dreaming?'

'No, no,' said Hanna soothingly. 'Not dreaming. We're just looking after you. You're not very well, and we want you to come and lie down.'

'Lie down indeed!' said Flip, pulling his shawl round him. 'I'm not going to get out of this chair, I tell you! Leave me alone!'

'Just let me unwind this hot shawl then,' begged Sally, trying to pull it off.

Flip knew what would happen if that came off, and showed him to be not an old rabbit, but a young bunny.

He made a growling noise and jerked his head back.

'I've got a terrible temper,' he shouted, 'so don't make me lose it! I'm a dreadful fellow when I'm roused, *though* I'm old. I *won't* have my shawl taken off!'

Dinky and Sally and Hanna looked at him in alarm.

'Yes, it's very bad sunstroke,' whispered Hanna. 'I'll get Hickory Hare, my husband, to come and hold him while I put some ice on his head. Stay here for a minute.'

She tiptoed out of the room and brought Hickory back with her. He held Flip firmly whilst Hanna tied a big lump of ice on his head. Flip

was so hot that the ice melted and ran in little cold streams down his neck. It was frightfully uncomfortable. But he didn't dare to struggle too much in case his shawl came off.

'Oh dear!' he thought. 'Why on earth did I let Binkle dress me up like this? I might have known trouble would come. Whatever is Binkle doing, anyway?'

Binkle at that very moment was hurrying back to where he had left Flip. He had gone to a greengrocer's and bought two fat turnips, which both he and Flip *loved* to eat raw, and then he had gone into a lemonade shop, sat down on a chair, and ordered two glasses of lemonade with parsley floating in it.

But when Rixie Rat brought it to him, he was fast asleep! He had put a pound out on the table, so she took it, and didn't wake him.

And when he *did* wake up, my goodness! he *was* in a state!

'Whatever will poor old Flip be thinking!' he groaned. He drank one glass of lemonade, picked up the other, and ran off.

But when he got to his pictures. Flip wasn't there! Binkle rubbed his eyes, twitched his nose, and flapped his ears, but no, Flip still wasn't there!

'But where *can* he have gone to?' marvelled Binkle. 'The chair's gone too. It can't have gone away by itself. What a mystery! Oh, well I may as well drink this lemonade before I look for him!'

He drank it, and sat down to think.

'Flip can't be trusted by himself,' he said at last. 'I oughtn't to have left him. Perhaps he got tired and went home.'

This seemed to Binkle to be the only explanation of Flip's mysterious disappearance. So after a while he packed up his pictures and trotted off towards Bumble Bee Common.

When he got there he sniffed at the turnips inside the bag.

'Flip doesn't deserve any for scooting off like that,' he decided. 'And I'm hungry, so I'll just sit down here and eat them.'

He sat down and began munching, feeling quite sure Flip must be waiting for him at Heather Cottage.

But Flip wasn't. He was still in Hanna's sitting-room, getting in

a worse and worse temper. He growled and fidgeted and flapped his ears and jiggled his chair until Hanna and Sally grew alarmed.

'I don't like it,' whispered Sally. 'Perhaps he's mad and hasn't got a sunstroke after all.'

'Perhaps so,' answered Hanna. 'What about fetching Wily Weasel over from Oak Tree Town? He'll find out where he belongs to, and take him back.'

Flip caught just two words of Hanna's whispering – and they were 'Wily Weasel,' the name of his enemy, the policeman of Oak Tree Town.

It was too much for Flip. He gave a terrified yell, leapt from his chair, and jumped straight out of the open window into the street! Up the road he tore, his

blue shawl flapping behind him like a flag!

'Oh! oh!' shrieked Hanna and Sally and Dinky in fright.

'Oh, look at him! Look at him!' gasped Sally in amazement. 'Would you believe that an old rabbit could jump and run like that?'

'He *must* be mad!' said Dinky nervously. 'It's a good thing he's gone!'

'What a surprising thing!' said Hanna Hare, fanning herself and panting a little from the shock. 'I wonder who he is and where he lives?'

Flip tore on up the street, scaring everybody he met. He was dreadfully angry – angry with Binkle for deserting him, frightened that Wily Weasel might catch him, and terribly uncomfortable in his shawl.

He stopped when he came to Bumble Bee Common and began to unwrap his shawl. Suddenly he heard a little humming sound near by. He peeped round a tree to see who it was.

It was Binkle – Binkle, eating a large turnip and humming cheerfully!

Flip was so furious that for once he forgot to be a meek little bunny, and he gave a tremendous yell and pounced on Binkle.

Binkle dropped his turnips and gave a howl of terror at the sight of Flip with ice on his head. Then Flip was on top of him and in two minutes he was thoroughly shaken and scolded.

'That'll teach you to leave me tied up in a wheelchair!' said Flip fiercely. 'Now I'm going to take the turnips and have a good feast by myself at Heather Cottage. *And don't you dare to come near till I've finished! Oh! and here's a present for you.*'

Flip took some ice from his head and slipped it down Binkle's neck!

Then the indignant little rabbit stalked off – and Binkle was so surprised that he didn't even dare to follow him!

CHAPTER 12

Binkle Gets a Dreadful Shock

Binkle and Flip had nothing to eat. Their larder was empty, and they were dreadfully hungry.

'Nobody will give us any work,' sighed Binkle. 'They all seem cross about something or other.'

Flip looked very gloomy.

'*Nobody* wants us,' he said. 'I've a good mind to go out and get lost and never come back. Perhaps Oak Tree Town would be sorry then.'

Binkle sighed – then he frowned – then he chuckled, jumped up and slapped Flip on the back.

'Binkle, *don't* do that!' said Flip angrily. 'I keep telling you not to. And if it means you've got an idea, just keep it to yourself. Flapping and slapping about like that!'

'But Flip, this is *your* idea,' began Binkle. 'I think if you went out and got lost, and then got captured by some foxes, who said they wouldn't let you go unless we gave them cabbages and things, I'd get Oak Tree Town to give them, don't you see?'

'No, I don't see at all,' answered Flip crossly. 'I'm certainly not going to be so silly as to get captured by foxes.'

'No, not *really*,' said Binkle excitedly. 'You could go and hide some-

where, Flip, and I'd write letters to Herbert and all the others, saying you were captured by foxes who wanted food to let you go. I'd collect the food and pretend to take it to the foxes, and you'd come along home and we'd eat it all ourselves.'

Flip, seeing that he wasn't *really* to be captured by the foxes, thought it wasn't such a bad idea.

'I'll go straightaway and hide now in the old hollow oak tree in Cuckoo Wood,' said Flip. 'You must hurry up with your letter writing, Binkle, because it's not very comfortable there, and I shan't want to stay there too long.'

'I'll write the letters now,' said Binkle. 'Goodbye, Flip! Come out of the oak tree when you hear me whistle.'

Flip scuttled off, climbed into the hollow tree, and settled down.

Binkle wrote three letters – one to Herbert Hedgehog, one to Wily Weasel, and one to Sammy Squirrel. They were all the same.

> *We have captured Flip Bunny, but we will let him go free if you will give six cabbages, six lettuces, and six turnips to Binkle Bunny to bring to us tomorrow afternoon in Cuckoo Wood in exchange for Flip.*
> *With kind regards from*
> *Three Foxes.*

'There!' said Binkle, licking the envelopes with his little pink tongue. 'There! Now when Wily, Herbert, and Sammy give me the things, I'll pretend I'm taking them to the foxes, but really I'll go and whistle to Flip, and when he jumps out of the oak tree, we'll have a jolly good feast.'

He popped the letters into Wily's, Herbert's, and Sammy's letter boxes that night, then back to Heather Cottage he went, and got into bed, chuckling to think of the cabbages, lettuces, and turnips he and Flip would have next day.

When Herbert and Sammy read their letters that night they went straight to Wily Weasel, the policeman, about it, and found him frowning over the letter Binkle had left in his letter box.

'What *shall* we do?' said Sammy. 'We can't let poor little Flip remain a prisoner.'

'We must certainly give Binkle Bunny the cabbages and things tomorrow to set Flip free,' said Herbert.

Wily Weasel frowned harder.

'I'm very worried,' he said. 'I think I shall go up to Cuckoo Wood myself tonight, and warn anyone I see there that bad foxes are about, in case anybody else gets captured.'

He put his helmet over his sharp ears, and went out, leaving Sammy and Herbert to talk over their letters.

It was very dark in Cuckoo Wood and nobody was about at all. Wily went along, quietly whistling to himself, thinking about poor Flip Bunny.

Suddenly, to his enormous astonishment, he heard a voice just by him say, 'Is that you, Binkle?'

Wily stopped and looked round. He swung his lantern here and there, but nobody was lurking among the trees. He leaned against a big oak tree and waited. He heard nothing and began to think he must have been mistaken. He pursed up his whiskered mouth, and began quietly whistling again.

'*Binkle!*' said a voice so close to him that he jumped. A head poked out of the hollow oak tree and a nose sniffed into his ear. 'Why have you come whistling round here tonight? Have you brought any cabbages?'

'Oho!' thought Wily to himself, as he recognised Flip's voice, 'so those letters were all a trick of Binkle's. Oho!'

He suddenly turned, caught hold of Flip's collar and swung him out of the tree on to the ground.

'Now!' he said, flashing his lantern on to the astonished rabbit, 'just tell me what you're doing here, Flip?'

Flip was too surprised to answer for a moment. He had quite thought it was Binkle he had heard whistling to him. He couldn't think *what* to say!

'I – I've been captured by foxes,' he stammered at last.

'Oh, *have* you?' snorted Wily disbelievingly. 'Well, why didn't you escape?'

'I – I – didn't think of it!' said poor Flip. 'Binkle's going to rescue me tomorrow.'

'Well, I'm going to rescue you instead,' said Wily, 'and you're going to come along with me. I see through the trick you and Binkle have played, and I'm going to play a little trick on Binkle while you're safely locked up in Oak Tree Town.'

He tied Flip's paws together, and roped him to a tree. Then he felt for a pencil and his notebook. He wrote a note and pinned it on the tree. This is what it said:

Ha! Ha! We have really captured Flip, and when he's fattened up, we'll eat him. Thank you for him, Binkle. If you want him back, perhaps we might exchange him for twenty cabbages, twenty lettuces, and twenty turnips. Come tonight and see.
From Three Fierce Foxes.

'That'll give Binkle a shock!' grinned Wily. 'When he reads that he'll think you really *have* been captured, Flip. I wonder what he'll do!'

Flip was too miserable to answer. Wily unroped him and together the two went through the wood to Oak Tree Town, where Wily locked Flip safely up for the night.

After that he went to see Herbert and Sammy, and with many chuckles told them what he had done.

'We'll give Binkle a regular fright tomorrow,' he laughed.

'And mind! When he comes begging for cabbages and things, don't give him any, and tell everyone else not to, either. Binkle must have a proper punishment this time.'

Next morning Binkle thought he would pop up to the hollow oak tree in Cuckoo Wood and tell Flip he had written and delivered the letters.

So off he went, gaily humming to himself. he whistled as he came near the oak tree, expecting Flip to pop his head out. But he didn't.

'Perhaps he's asleep,' said Binkle. Then he caught sight of the notice Wily had pinned up and he went to read it.

'Oh! Oh! Oh!' he yelled when he had read it. 'Flip's really been captured. Oh! Oh! Oh! What shall I do? Poor, poor Flip! Oh, those horrid foxes! Oh, I must really go and beg for twenty cabbages, lettuces, and turnips. Oh my! Oh my!'

He peeped in the hollow tree and saw it was empty. Then, with flapping ears and staring eyes, he raced through the wood into Oak Tree Town.

He saw Mowdie Mole and Sammy Squirrel in Herbert Hedgehog's front garden.

Breathlessly he rushed up to them.

'Help!' he cried, 'Flip's been captured by foxes. They say they'll eat him unless we take them twenty cabbages, turnips, and lettuces. Oh, quick, Herbert, let me dig up some of yours?'

'Certainly *not*,' said Herbert. 'My cabbages are much too valuable.'

'You horrid thing!' cried Binkle. 'You'll give me some of yours, won't you, Sammy and Mowdie!'

But Sammy and Mowdie refused, too.

'No,' they said, 'certainly not.'

Binkle couldn't believe his ears. How could anyone be so unkind when poor Flip was captured by foxes?

He rushed to Dilly Duck's and begged her for some of her lettuces.

'No, Binkle,' said Dilly, who was usually the soul of kindness. 'I can't spare any today.'

'Oh, *please*, Dilly?' begged Binkle. 'Just to save Flip!'

'If Flip and you were good bunnies,' began Dilly, 'perhaps I might have given you some. But you're not!'

'Oh, I'll always be good now, I'll always be good,' cried Binkle. But it wasn't any use, Dilly wouldn't change her mind.

Binkle went to Susie Squirrel and to Derry Dormouse, to Riggles Rat and to Wily Weasel, and to everyone else he knew. But not one single person would

let him have any cabbages, lettuces, or turnips.

'This is my punishment for being naughty,' sighed poor Binkle. 'Oh, dear, dear! To think poor Flip's been captured like that, all because I had a naughty idea. Oh, if ever I get him back, I'll never be bad again, never!'

He sat on the ground and thought what he could do for Flip. He frowned hard and two tears flopped on to the ground.

'I know!' said Binkle at last. 'I'll go to the tree myself tonight, and offer to go with the foxes in exchange for Flip's freedom. I'm fat and plump and they'd much rather have *me*.'

So the brave little bunny got up and ran off. On the way he met Wily Weasel, who wanted to know where he was going, and Binkle told him. Wily said nothing and went on his way, leaving Binkle to go to the oak tree.

But Wily was thinking hard. He was astonished that Binkle should have thought of giving himself up for Flip, and he was very pleased. He hurried into Oak Tree Town and called on all the folk there, telling them what Binkle was going to do.

'Binkle's braver and better than

we thought, for all his naughtiness,' said Wily. 'If only we could persuade him to be good and use his clever brains to help us instead of playing tricks on us, he would be of great use to Oak Tree Town.'

'What are you going to do about Flip?' asked Herbert.

'This is what I've planned,' said Wily with a chuckle. 'We'll all go up to Cuckoo Wood with Flip. When we see Binkle there, I'll call out as if I were a fox, and ask him questions. We'll see how he answers them, and if he answers properly, we'll untie Flip and let him go back to Binkle.'

So off they all went, taking poor frightened Flip with them. Wily hid behind a tree as soon as he saw Binkle and waved the others away.

Binkle was standing there alone, looking about for the foxes.

'Foxes!' he called, 'foxes!'

'Yes!' answered Wily, making poor Binkle jump in fright.

'I haven't got the things you wanted,' said Binkle in a trembling voice. 'So I've brought myself. Will you have me instead of Flip? I'm much fatter.'

'Are you a good or a naughty bunny?' asked Wily, still pretending to be a fox.

'A naughty one,' answered Binkle, 'but I wish I hadn't been, for then I wouldn't have got Flip into trouble.'

'Do you want to be good now?' asked Wily, thoroughly enjoying himself, and grinning at all the others listening.

'Yes, I do,' answered Binkle, 'and I'll promise to be good always if only you'll let Flip go free.'

Wily turned to the others.

'Do you hear that?' he whispered. 'We'll let Flip go to him, and then we'll tell him we'll keep him to his promise.'

Flip's paws were untied and he scampered to Binkle, who could hardly believe his eyes and hugged him as if he would squeeze him to death.

Then to his tremendous surprise all the others came crowding up.

'Now, Binkle!' said Wily, 'we've heard your promise, and we don't mean you to break it. You must always be good now you've got Flip back again.'

Binkle stared in amazement.

'Is it all a trick?' he asked at last.

'It's a trick that came out of *your* trick,' said Wily, and told him all that had happened.

Binkle was too thankful to know that Flip really was safe, and that he himself wasn't going to be captured by foxes, to say anything cross or unkind. He really *did* feel he'd never be naughty again and, of course, if *he* wasn't, Flip wouldn't be.

Sammy Squirrel kindly asked both bunnies to go to supper with him, and as they were really too hungry for anything, they went.

That was just six months ago, and as far as I know, Binkle has kept his word. But I am told he is already beginning to find it rather a nuisance to be good. So I shouldn't be at all surprised to hear that he and Flip have become bad bunnies once again.

I hope not, but if they do, you may be sure I'll let you know.